# Fights for Furry Rights

ROS ASQUITH

HarperCollins *Children's Books*

*With Very Extremely special thanks to*
*Purrrrfect editor Stella Paskins and*
*Wooftastic designer Elorine Grant for turning my*
*ravings and doodles into a REAL BOOK.*

First published in Great Britain by HarperCollins **Children's Books** 2007
Harper Collins **Children's Books** is a division of HarperCollins **Publishers** Ltd
77-85 Fulham Palace Road, Hammersmith, London, W6 8JB

www.harpercollinschildrensbooks.co.uk

1



ISBN 13: 978 0 00 722359 6
ISBN 10: 0 00 722359 5

Printed and bound in Great Britain by
Clays Ltd, St Ives plc

# Chapter 1

"You know, those puppies are very sweet, but they're getting bigger by the minute," Mum said as she watched my little brother Tomato trying to get two spoonfuls of Krispy Popsicles into his mouth at once. If she was thinking there wasn't much difference between Tomato and the puppies eating breakfast, I could see her point. But I knew what was coming next so I got ready to wail in my best tragic wailing manner.

"We really must find homes for them. The time has come," concluded Mum.

"Noooooooooooooooo!" I wailed tragically. "You said we could keep them all!"

"When?" asked Mum.

"I can't remember, but you definitely did. Didn't she?"

I turned to my little brother Tomato for support, but he now had his face stuck right inside the bowl of Krispy Popsicles. He

looked like he was trying to lick the pattern of Dalmatian puppies off the rim.

"But this is the puppies' home! You can't send them away! They might be made into fur coats!"

"Don't be ridiculous, Trixie, that sort of thing doesn't happen any more."

"Any more? You mean it really did happen?" I said. "It wasn't just something that happened in stories?" I was shocked.

Dad came in, carrying a plank. He's always carrying planks. He likes fixing things around the house. It makes him feel useful, and the noise he makes hammering and drilling stops him from noticing anything he doesn't want to hear – like family rows, questions about whether he's done the shopping, or if he has any money for once. That kind of thing.

"It's true. You couldn't keep a cat for five minutes when my dad was a lad," he said, knocking the Krispy Popsicles off the table with the back of the plank. Tomato howled indignantly and the puppies all yapped as they fell over each other to grab some. Not that they liked it much when they got it. "Blokes would drive round at dead of night and catch 'em in nets. Next thing you know they'd be fur hats. The cats, not the blokes."

"Don't be silly. And shush, you'll scare Tomato," Mum said.

Tomato didn't seem very scared. He was dropping Krispy Popsicles on the puppies' shiny noses and chanting: "Blokes in coats, cats in hats, dads and lads, poos in loos," while sticking his tongue out in the effort to direct a Krispy Popsicle at Big Fattypuff's ear. Big Fattypuff is one of the sweetest of the puppies, not that they aren't all sweet of course.

"Remember to be home by four in case I'm late back," Mum said, getting up. "That woman who might buy Gran's china is coming round this afternoon – somebody's got to do something to raise some extra money in this household. One day we might be able to afford to get the roof fixed."

**"Cats and prats, purrs and furs, paws on floors, dads are mad," Tomato carried on.**

I followed Mum around the kitchen as she got ready to go to school. She's a teacher. "How can you go on about the boring old roof and boring old china when the puppies' lives are at stake?"

"Don't be such a drama queen, Trixie."

"You don't care!" I shouted at Mum's fast-disappearing form. "Harpo's their mum! She'll be brokenhearted if her puppies leave home! You wouldn't like it if someone stole YOUR children!"

Mum glanced first at me, then at Tomato, who seemed to have more cereal stuck to his outside than he had managed to cram into his inside. "I wouldn't bank on that," she said, whisking out of the door.

All this worry about the puppies made me late for school, of course. I slunk into class and, risking the evil x-ray eye of our demon teacher, Warty-Beak, I passed an anguished note to my best friend Dinah.

I watched Dinah reading it, then passing it to Chloe, my other best friend.

Chloe was busy checking her new pet ant that she carries around everywhere in a matchbox, so it took her a few seconds before she realised what Dinah was doing. But when they had both read my note they turned to look at me with agonised faces contorted in woe, as though they had just read about the End of the World. It was very comforting.

Warty-Beak was droning on about some project or other we all had to get finished by yesterday, but I couldn't concentrate. All I could think about were Little Marigold with her fluffy paws, Cheeky Eric with his naughty ways, Big Fattypuff with his huge soft eyes like saucers of honey, Tiny Gertrude with her

curly-wurly tail and, worst of all, my beloved Bonzo, King of my Heart.

How would I sleep without Bonzo on my bed? And what about Harpo, their mum, who had brought them all up and cared for them since the day they were born? I must tell you that if I were a crying sort of person, which I most definitely am not, I might have shed a tear there and then on my empty page.

"Away with the fairies again, Patricia Tempest? You appear not to have written down a single word."

I jumped. The gimletty eye of Warty bored like a dentist's drill into the depths of my soul.

"Sorry, Warty... er, Mr Wartover," I stuttered. "My pen's dried up."

"The originality of your excuses appears to have dried up too, Patricia," Warty sneered. This

is the kind of sneaky thing he loves saying, and he looks all pleased afterwards, as if he's expecting a round of applause. Everybody groans of course.

Warty returned to the front of the class with a gloaty, beaky snigger.

"I want this project to be your very best work, as we are going to make a special display of it for parents' evening. It must be at least six pages of writing with some nice illustrations. AND, as this is a very special parents' evening, to celebrate the twentieth anniversary of St Aubergine's Primary School, you are all, in your groups, going to present your projects with a little speech."

A chorus of further groans ran round the class. Groan groan groan groanetty groan. Warty paid no attention and ploughed on.

"The title, for those of you who may not have heard the first time," he continued, glaring at me, "is 'The Pride of Bottomley'."

Just to put you in the picture, this is not some weird school anti-thin-awareness project to get us all to be proud of having bottoms. It's a project

about the town we live in, which is called Bottomley. You might wonder how anybody could hope to get taken seriously in life coming from a place called that, and I would agree with you, but that's another subject. You probably know the kind of school project I mean. It's one of those no-brainers where they get you to walk up and down the high street with a calculator, count the number of lorries going past and divide them by the number of fish and chip shops, that kind of thing.

"Why doesn't Warty give us something interesting to do, like the Amazon Rainforest?" I muttered as we filed out after what felt like hours and hours.

"Yeah, or how many heads got cut off in the French Revolution?" said Sumil, bashing Dennis with his school bag. Dennis bashed him back. It's the way boys show they're friends.

Me and Dinah and Chloe headed for the quiet corner, but my archenemies Ghastly Grey Griselda and Orrible Orange Orson had got there first and were busy tormenting small shy Year Threes.

They'd emptied out their bags on to the ground and were making stupid jokes about the contents.

"EEeww, a HANKY! Is that for mopping up when you wet yourself?"

"Yeeech, a MARMITE SANDWICH! Marmite's made from dog poo, you know!"

That kind of thing.

"We ought to help," said Chloe, stepping behind me and Dinah. Dinah's almost taller than Grey Griselda and Orange Orson put together. And Chloe, for that matter. So we went over and glared at them.

"Haven't you got anything better to do?" Dinah asked sarkily, drawing herself up to her full supermodel height.

"Like using old ladies as footballs?" I added.

Ghastly Grey Griselda and Orrible Orange Orson grumbled a bit but slouched off. We shooed the Year Threes away and sat down.

"Ohmigod, I can't believe your mum's going to sell the puppies," Dinah said. "Doesn't she have a heart?"

"It's made of stone," I said gloomily.

Griselda and Orange Orson hadn't gone far. Griselda has big flapping ears that always hear anything you don't want her to. She started carrying on at us, though obviously ready to run if Dinah or me took a step in their direction.

"Sell those mongrels? You'd be lucky to get a fiver for the lot!" she hooted. "Unless you're selling them to make school dinners..."

We took a step and they ran for it.

"She's got a point though," Dinah said. "No offence, but don't people only pay money for pedigree dogs?"

"That's not the point," I said furiously. "The point is my mum wants to get rid of the puppies. So she'll advertise them and then people will come and take them away. Anyway they're not mongrels, they're crossbreeds."

"They don't look very cross to me. They look cute," Chloe said.

For someone who's a definite brainiac, Chloe has some strange gaps in her education.

"I'm sure you could sell them. Their dad is very posh, isn't he?" she continued.

This was true: the puppies' father, Lorenzo, the Dog-Next-Door and the love of Harpo's life, is a red setter of amazing pedigree and Mrs Next-Door is always boasting about the prizes he wins at posh dog shows.

"Do you think puppies really get turned into food?" I asked, feeling a jelly-leg attack coming on. Griselda always manages to say the one thing that really gets to you. I have no regrets about that hot chilli sauce I put in her stupid lunch box with fairies on. Or the big fat slug. I hope it ate her stupid sandwiches.

"There are countries where people eat dogs, and ants too, covered in chocolate,"' said Chloe, quickly checking her matchbox and looking at her pet ant anxiously. "I don't think we do it here..."

"But we've got no idea what they put in

hamburgers or sausages," I said.

"Please, no lectures about how we should all be vegetarians," said Dinah. "But we've got to find a way of keeping the puppies safe. We have to have a brainstorm."

Dinah goes on about this all the time at the moment, ever since our headteacher Mrs Hedake told us how a brainstorm works. Apparently, if you have a problem, you should get a big bit of paper and just write the first words that come into your head. Then after five minutes you will have a solution. Hedake said it was better still if you did it with a friend because they would have different ideas. Of course, all the Year Sixes giggled and nudged about what kind of words they would write down, but Dinah was convinced. She had used it that very same evening for persuading her dad to let her stay up and watch a scary film.

So me and Chloe and Dinah sat under the tree in the playground and scribbled away.

This is what we wrote:

We got stuck after that. When I looked up there was a tall, lonely looking girl I hadn't seen before moping about on the other side of the tree, looking at me in a shy but friendly way.

"Hi," she said, smiling hopefully. She had the most enormous braces I've ever seen on her teeth. It was like looking at the front of a car.

"Hi. Are you new?" I said.

"Yeah, we've just moved here," she said. "What are you doing?"

"Brainstorming," said Dinah, not looking much like somebody who wanted to be a friend.

"What's that?" asked the girl.

"It's where you say the first things that come into your head and it gives you the answer," Chloe explained.

"I've tried doing that in exams," said the girl, rather sadly. "But I don't think it works. What are you doing it about?"

"Saving my puppies from being made into coats or sausages," I said. "Any ideas?"

"Oh, yes!" said the girl. "I love animals! My dad's got an amazing dog who does tricks—"

"Send the lickle puppeees to the science lab, make them smoke fags till they gags, then their fluffy tails won't wag!" interrupted the voice of of Orrible Orange Orson, who had sneaked up on us again.

I lost my rag and went for him. Dinah and Chloe hauled me off.

"Who cares anyway?" laughed Orson, dusting

himself down and backing away. "They're only dumb animals."

"You should know!" I yelled after him.

He turned round and gave me a sign that I can't repeat in a family book, but Dinah and I gave it him back, and Chloe half did, before going red and putting her hand in her pocket instead.

"What a loser," I said, panting. "He's never even seen my puppies. Why doesn't he get a life?"

"That *is* his life," Dinah said. "He's very happy with it."

"Where's that girl gone?" said Chloe, looking around. "She seemed nice."

"I think Orson scared her off," Dinah said. "Who wouldn't run away, seeing his ugly face? Anyway, where were we?"

I looked glumly at the brainstorming.

"Who's Cheeky Eric?" asked Chloe.

"He's a puppy! You don't even know their names. That shows how much you care."

"Lay off, Trix," said Dinah. "The only one you

go on about is Bonzo. The others are always curled up on top of Harpo and it's pretty hard to tell them apart."

"But they've all got amazingly different characters," I said. "Just like people. Eric's mischievous and cheeky, Marigold's cute and pretty like that actress who came to do puppet workshop, Fattypuff has big film-star eyes and is incredibly lazy, Gertrude is shy and kind, like Chloe, and her tail is just like a Curly-Wurly. And Bonzo..."

I tailed off. I could see I was losing them. It was a bit like Mum's friend who pops in for a "quick cup of tea" and then bores on and on for hours about her horrible dribbling squawking baby.

"Of course, you never see them as individuals cos you're not there all the time like me. And Harpo rules them with a paw of iron," I added.

"Can anyone remember what any of this means?" said Dinah, turning our brainstorm paper upside down as though it might make more sense that way. "Looks like some of that poetry my mum writes when she's in a mood."

"Well, BEG and PLEAD were about trying to change my parents' mind," I said. "Oh, yeah, and DAD!!!! was because I can usually get round him so I had a brainwave of persuading him..."

"And PLAGUE and BITE were about telling people the puppies are dangerous, so no one will want them," said Chloe.

"Excellent!" said Dinah. "That's a good start. We'll begin with you trying to persuade your dad to make your mum keep the puppies. If she won't relent, you'll do everything you can to make sure no one wants the puppies anyway." She squinted at the piece of paper. "Oh yes, and if that doesn't

work, we'll erm, either disguise the puppies as, erm, something else, or hide them, or run away from home with them! OK? This is the beginning of our campaign. We'll get lots of support to save them from experiments. Let's do a petition this evening and call it Puppies Are People Too."

"YES. If we can persuade the whole neighbourhood your parents are trying to sell the puppies into slavery, we can probably get the RSPCA to help, or the police," said Chloe.

"Don't overdo it. If my folks go to jail, who'll buy the dog food?"

"Of course, you couldn't get anyone interested if you'd only lost your pet ant," Chloe added sadly. I think since her last ant got hoovered up she is taking her new one, Anty, too seriously. She needs a new interest. And she needs to stop worrying about School.

"Maybe," Chloe went on, "we could tie this in with our Pride of Bottomley project."

There! What did I tell you??

"You have to be kidding, Chloe," said Dinah,

putting an arm around her. "Saving the Puppies will be an adventure. The Pride of Bottomley isn't an adventure; it's a punishment."

"But Trixie's puppies are part of the Pride of Bottomley," Chloe protested. "She's proud of them. We are too, even if we don't know all their names."

"Or which one can play the piano with its back paws, and which one can do Sudoko and speak Chinese," cackled Dinah.

"Shut up," I said. But an idea was beginning to hatch somewhere in the murky depths of my brain.

"We could bring in the science lab at Mandleton, where they do Animal Experiments and Testing," Chloe said, getting excited. "That would come under 'The Shame of Bottomley'."

"Yeah," said Dinah. "Animal rights. Save the Snail."

I was cheered up, despite Dinah's jokes. I knew that with Dinah and Chloe on my side, the puppies were in with a chance. And we were getting our Warty project done at the same time!

But when I got home, a nasty shock awaited me. A very flash car was parked outside the gate. And a very flash woman with bright pink hair and stiletto heels to match was teetering out of our house, carrying an enormous box and squealing to the driver, "They're purrrrfect. Exactly what we were after! I'm taking them all!"

I couldn't believe it! Mum had only just that morning mentioned the pups might have to go and she'd found a buyer already! They were going out of my life, squashed inside a cardboard box!

I flung myself in the way ofthe horrendous pink witch.

"Over my dead body!" I squeaked.

Unfortunately, what with the

stiletto heels and the surprise at seeing a tiny furious girl barring her way, the pink witch tottered, squawked and then seemed to go in four different directions at once. One leg went south, one leg went north, her arms went out sideways, her pink hair blew off in a gust of wind revealing some quite ordinary hair underneath, and the box of puppies went soaring into the air.

"Ohmigod! The pups!" I squealed, leaping up to catch it on its way down.

"Ohmigod! The pups!" screamed Wigless Witch, struggling to get up and catch the box as well.

We collided of course, and the box landed on our heads with a horrible crashing, tinkling sound. Then it slid to the ground and split open.

I stared. There were no bruised, whimpering, terrified puppies to be seen.

There *were* a lot of cups and saucers and plates. Or what had once been cups and saucers and plates. What had once been, in fact, the

THIS SIDE UP

valuable tea set belonging to my gran that Mum was selling for a lot of money. Even I could see that no amount of superglue was going to save it.

I looked at Wigless Witch accusingly. Why had she made me do that? Hadn't she yelled "Ohmigod! The pups!" when she dropped them?

Obviously not, said another part of my brain. Obviously she'd said "cups".

Dad came out looking miserable. He doesn't really do cross, my dad. My mum does cross, but Dad does sad, which makes you feel worse. He took a wad of cash out of his pocket and picked up the witch's once-pink-and-now-mud-spattered wig, and solemnly returned both to her. I looked shamefully down at the ground.

I was well and truly in the dog house. Bonzo came to comfort me as I lay on my Bed of Pain, but his warm furry presence only succeeded in reminding me of what I was about to lose… I didn't have the heart to nag Dad any more about the puppies. He said Mum would see the funny side of it eventually, but I couldn't see how.

Dinah and Chloe both rang me during the evening. I was supposed to be in solitary confinement, but Mum had either forgotten or relented, most probably the first. Dinah was her usual bouncy self, said it would have all blown over by morning, which I doubted. Chloe was sweet, and talked to me about the puppies as if they were hers too.

"I don't want them to get turned into coats, Chloe," I sniffled to her. "Tell me they won't be."

"They won't. We'll find a way," Chloe said. "Don't you worry. Most people usually

buy puppies to play with, not to make into coats."

"But I can't bear to lose them!"

"No. And of course..." She hesitated.

"What?"

"It's obviously a bad world out there for little animals. I saw a notice pinned on a tree in our street from somebody looking for their missing cat. That's the third one I've seen round here in a week. Strange, isn't it?"

"Yes," I said glumly, remembering Dad's words from this morning. "Thanks, Chloe."

"Don't mention it. Sleep tight."

I didn't, of course.

# Chapter 2

The very next morning, Mum was huddled over the kitchen table scribbling on a piece of paper. When I came in, she covered it up in a sneaky manner.

"What are you doing?" I asked.

"Writing to Father Christmas," Mum said. "He's the only one left to turn to since you've smashed our only means of raising a bit of extra cash."

"I'm really sorry about that," I said, trying to put an arm round her. "I said I was sorry. It was an accident."

I could see the edge of the piece of paper Mum had tried to cover up. It said DELICIOUS PUPPIES FOR.

"Delicious puppies for what?" I demanded, wrestling with Mum to pull the paper out. No prizes for guessing what it said.

DELICIOUS PUPPIES FOR SALE

"MUM! We haven't discussed this properly! You said you were going to have another think about it!"

Mum sighed. "No, I didn't. And if I had, what happened yesterday settles it. Look, Trix, you're being really silly about this. All puppies have to leave home and we've already kept them too long. They'll eat us out of house and home – and who's going to take SIX huge dogs for a walk? They won't be puppies for ever you know. Soon they'll be huge, like Harpo. Just imagine!"

I looked at humungous Harpo. It was hard to

imagine six of her in one room, but I managed. "It'll save on electricity," I said hopefully.

"What ARE you talking about?" Mum looked exasperated.

"Well, I read that seven people in a room make so much heat you don't have to have the central heating on. So six Harpos would keep the kitchen cosy all through winter..."

"What about all the rest of the house?" Mum asked, rather sarkily. I couldn't think of an answer to that.

"I haven't got time to argue about this and I'm surprised you're worrying about the bills for the first time in your life, especially after what happened yesterday."

"But you CAN'T write that!" I shrieked. "Not DELICIOUS puppies!"

"What's wrong with it?"

"They'll be bought by dog thieves and baked in a pie!"

Mum struggled not to laugh. "Maybe delicious is a bit silly, but everyone always puts 'adorable' or 'cute'. I wanted to make it different, so people would—"

"Be more likely to take them! Mum! We've raised them from the day they were born. How can you be so UNFEELING?"

But she was looking at her watch and scooping up Tomato and heading for the door.

"You're always in a hurry! There's never time for a proper conversation," I complained. Then, to make her feel really guilty, I added, "Except

you always have time to talk to parents at parents' evening, or the silly headmistress!"

"This isn't a conversation, Trix. That's when two people listen to each other. You're just trying to bully me into doing what you want. When you're a grown-up, you can decide to keep a hundred Harpos and their puppies if you want to, and pay for their food and vet bills and all the rest. But for now, I make the decisions. I will write out the advertisement tonight and it will be in the newsagent's window tomorrow, and that's final." And off she went.

**I turned to Dad, who was pretending to examine a tap.**

"Don't know why it's always dripping," he muttered when he caught me staring at him.

"It's not," I said. "You're just trying to keep out of the arguments as usual. Surely YOU don't want to sell the pups, do you?"

"Erm... um. Let's talk about it later. You'll be late for school."

It's always the same. School just plonks itself in the way of real life every single day. Horrible looming boring school with stupid sums and tests, and Orrible Orange Orson lurking in the toilets and Ghastly Grey Griselda waiting to slam doors on your fingers, and the gimletty laser-eye of Warty-Beak waiting to BORE a hole into your soul as if you are a useless worm. **I am going to create a world without school where children and puppies can run free and play all day and the streets are made of grass and sweeties grow on trees...**

On the way to school next day I kept seeing notices for lost cats stuck to lampposts.

"Do you think someone is cat-napping them and turning them into hats? Like when Grandad was a lad?" I asked Chloe later in the playground.

"I don't think so," she replied in her usual cautious way. "Although come to think of it..."

"What? Come to think of what?"

"The dog next door to us has gone missing."

"See? There's a pet-napper on the prowl! If Mum advertises the puppies it's like pointing an arrow straight at their hearts, saying 'Get your new fur coat here'!"

"But it's uncool to be seen in a fur coat these days, isn't it? What with Animal Rights and all. People in woolly hats with banners would chase them down the street calling them nasty names."

"What would they be doing in woolly hats?" I wondered. "They're from animals too."

"Well, they don't *have* to be in woolly hats," Chloe said. "Anyway, you just have to give sheep a haircut to get wool. You don't have to murder them. It's supportive. Probably Animal Rights people wear them to keep the sheep population in work."

"Fur coat people wouldn't worry about all that," I said. "You never see them walking down the street, or at the checkout or whatever. They're always behind darkened windows in a stretch limo."

"Aren't you two getting off the point?" said Dinah, who had joined us. "We need a plan. Where's your mum going to advertise the puppies?"

"Mr Drugg's noticeboard in his window," I told her. Mr Drugg was the newsagent and sweetie man, not that he is very sweet himself.

"OK," Dinah said. "Why don't we just go down there and hide it? Chloe could keep Mr Drugg talking, he likes her. She pretty much keeps his shop going all by herself."

Chloe gave Dinah an annoyed look. Well, as annoyed as she's capable of, which isn't very. "No good," she said. "Your mum would notice." (This would be Very Extremely soon, since Mum nips into Mr Drugg's on a daily basis.)

"What about putting a sign saying SOLD on top of it?" I suggested.

"No good," said Chloe again. "Your mum would see it and if the puppies weren't sold she'd know it was us."

We all shuffled about in silence, until Chloe squeaked, "I've got it! We'll change one digit of the phone number. It would be easy to change

1189 to 7189. And your mum won't notice for ages because the ad will still look nearly the same."

"Chloe, you are a GENIUS!"

Chloe went red-as-a-beetroot and gazed at her feet. "I don't know..." she murmured. "It's breaking the law, really."

"What law?" I demanded. "William The Conqueror's Sweetie Man Protection Act of 1071? There's no law that says you can get your head chopped off for making a mistake on an advert."

"Yes, but it's not a mistake, it's a scam by us. We'll be criminals," Chloe moaned.

"Look," Dinah said impatiently, "do we want to save these puppies or not? You can't make an omelet without breaking eggs."

Chloe and I looked blank.

"We're not making an omelet, we're saving my puppies," I said. "What are you talking about?"

"I don't know. It's something my dad says," Dinah replied. "Anyway," (she gave Chloe a big hug, which made her blush even more), "it's an amazing idea. I had exactly the same one at the same time, actually."

"Yeah, yeah," Chloe and I went. Dinah hates to be beaten at problem-solving.

I did a lot of nagging and persuading for the next two days, but on Saturday Mum put the card in the newsagent.

FIVE ADORABLE
RED SETTER/OLD ENGLISH SHEEPDOG CROSS
PUPPIES. EXCELLENT PEDIGREES.
GOOD HOMES ONLY.

Then she put in our phone number and, worst of all, stuck on a photo of the puppies that I had taken only last week! It was the cutest picture you could imagine. They were all brushed and combed and shampooed, and even sleepy old

Fattypuff looked alert, and Gertrude's tail was even curlier and wurlier than usual.

I gulped. It was really happening. I was going to lose the puppies. Unless Chloe's phone-number trick might just possibly work.

I made Mum put that bit about good homes in, even though it went against my better judgement to help with the horrible Advertisement of Doom. I also pointed out that the pedigree thingy on Harpo's side was not strictly true, i.e. a lie, since Mum first found Harpo abandoned in a park.

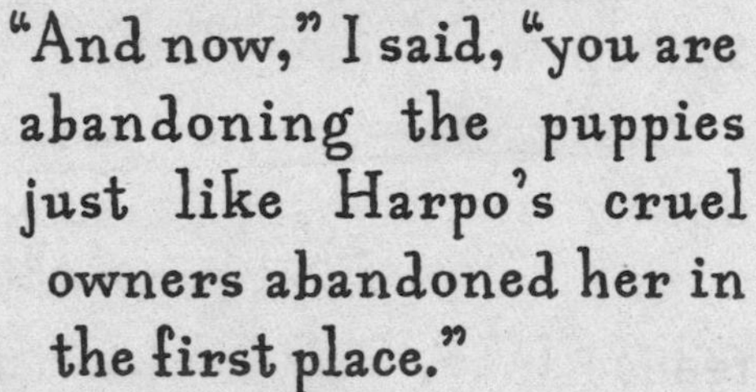

"And now," I said, "you are abandoning the puppies just like Harpo's cruel owners abandoned her in the first place."

"That's not fair," said Dad, coming into the room carrying three planks for protection. "They'll go to good homes."

"Let me at least keep Bonzo!" I wailed. I hadn't asked properly before because I thought it would be disloyal to the

other puppies. But the thought of losing Bonzo from my bed each night suddenly overwhelmed me.

Mum paused on her way to the door. "I'll think about it," she said.

Was this a ray of hope?

I rushed to ring Dinah.

"No, that's terrible," she said. "If they let you keep Bonzo it will let them off the hook. You are betraying the other puppies."

"Great. Now I am a traitor as well as the Saddest Person in the World."

"No, we can still stop this happening. Let's go down the newsagent and sabotage the ad."

"It sounds easy," I grumbled, "but how are we really going to do it? Old Drugg is the suspiciousest and most hawk-eyed person in the world, even if he's only got one eye that works. I just stroked a chocolate mouse in there once, right at the other side of the shop, and he made me buy it. He can see round corners."

"We'll find a way. Call Chloe and we'll go down there."

Half an hour later, me and Dinah and Chloe arrived at Mr Drugg's shop, armed with a black felt tip. He'd given Mum's disgustrous advert the very best place right in the middle of the noticeboard in the window. Big Fattypuff's saucer eyes gazed down at me, and I couldn't bear to look at Bonzo's furry little face, so I dived into the shop more determined than ever.

Mr Drugg has NOT MORE THAN TWO SCHOOL CHILDREN AT A TIME signs everywhere and shouts if you breathe on his biros. Luckily, though, he has a soft spot for Chloe who is his most regular customer. Sweeties are Mr Drugg's pride and joy. He has shelves and shelves full of them in old-fashioned huge glass jars – every kind you could wish for and a lot imported from abroad which you can't get anywhere else in Bottomley. It's weird, for a bloke who hates kids. He knows me and Dinah are Chloe's best friends, so he usually lets us stand quietly at the back of his shop while Chloe and he have long chats about which is best, fudge or marshmallows.

So, Chloe engaged him in a long conversation

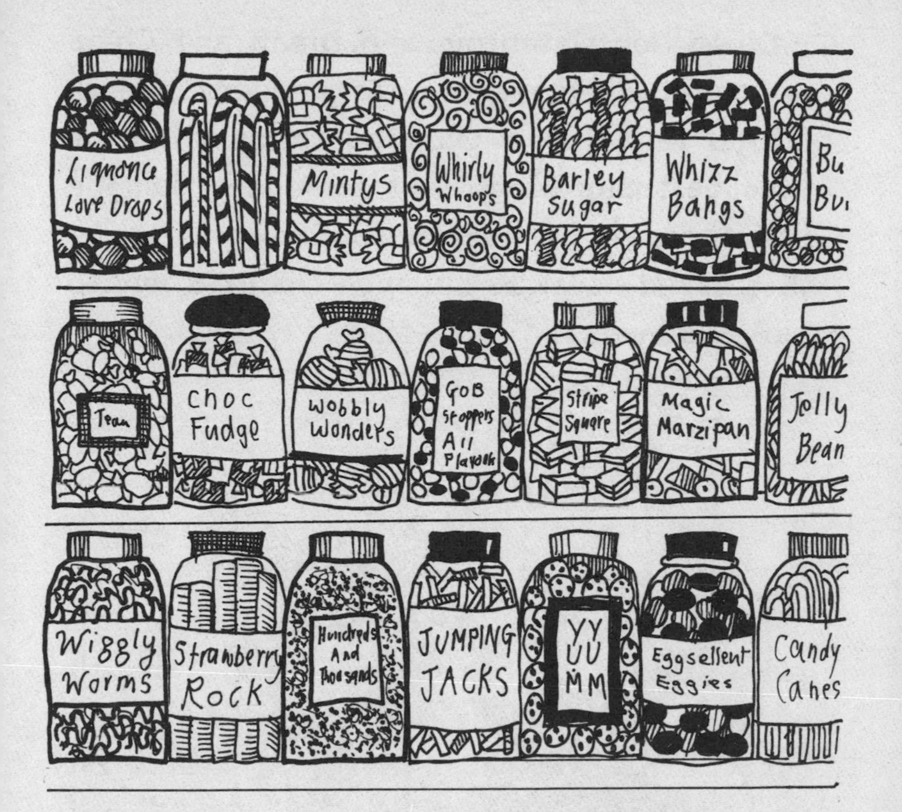


about the best brands of peppermint and whether the tongue-burning toffee twisters she'd ordered last week had come in yet and had he heard of the new multiflavoured sherbert from Taiwan? Chloe's a walking encyclopedia of sweets, and me and Dinah could see Mr Drugg was really enjoying himself talking to an expert.

Dinah leafed through magazines by the window to shield me from Drugg's demonic eye.

"All right, he's showing Chloe a box of Firebreathing Flogwobblers or something," Dinah giggled. "They're so strong he keeps them under lock and key in the back room, guarded by dogs."

"Never mind that," I hissed. "Shall I go for it?"

"It's now or never," Dinah said. "You could even draw a few fleas and fly-covered sores on that itsy-bitsy picture of the puppies, just to put people off." She was laughing so much now I thought old Drugg was bound to hear her, but his ears aren't as good as his one eye.

My hand slipped into the window display and I changed the phone number.

Chloe bought a ton of sweeties and we said goodbye very politely. Mr Drugg looked at us quite fondly as we scarpered.

"Even if we haven't saved them for ever," said Dinah, "it buys us some time."

But it seemed she was wrong.

When I got home, Mrs Next-Door was sitting in the kitchen with Lorenzo, the puppies' father and the Love of Harpo's Life. Mum was saying, "So I told her she could come any time today and see them all. She's the first person to ring, so I said she could take her pick."

I couldn't believe it. Someone had rung already and the ad had only been in the window for about an hour before we changed the phone number. Then I remembered the tea set. Maybe Mum was selling something else.

"Is that the puppies you're talking about?" I asked in a wobbly voice.

"Yes, isn't it brilliant? I only put that ad in shop this morning! But that picture you took was so gorgeous, we'll probably be swamped with calls!" said Mum brightly. "This lady who's coming wants more than one. And is even willing to pay money for them!"

"I'm not surprised by that," said Mrs Next-Door. "Some people might see them as mongrels, but any pup of Lorenzo's is bound to be special, isn't it Lorenzokins?" She stroked his slinky red coat and gave him a Doggy-Treat in front of Harpo and the puppies, who were looking at her all hopeful and wide-eyed.

But Mum had noticed my stricken face. "Trixie, she sounds very nice. Actually, she's rather posh, I think. Maybe she has a big country estate. The puppies will be able to run about in a rural paradise. She's called Lady Venus Goodchild, believe it or not."

"Sounds like some stupid bimbo in a James Bond film," I moaned.

"She might invite us to her lovely palatial home," trilled Mrs Next-Door, who talks like an article in *Hello!* She's an awful snob and thinks she is made for better things than a titchy house in Bottomley. She never comes round here usually.

"But if they go miles away, we won't even be able to visit them," I protested.

"She lives quite close. In Mandleton," said Mum.

And at that moment, the doorbell rang.

"Go and get that, Trix," Mum said.

As I opened the front door, my worst fears were realised. Into the house swept a nightmare vision, the most horrible looking woman I have ever seen. She was over two metres tall and two

metres wide, with staring eyes of a sickly greenish-yellow like a cat's or a tiger's. She had long red hair down to her knees and an enormous sticky red lipsticky mouth which she stretched wide open in what I supposed she thought was a smile, but with her rows of snaggly teeth she looked more like a crocodile eyeballing a tasty snack. She was dressed entirely in red. Scarlet boots, flame tights, maroon plastic mackintosh and a huge red feather boa that looked like a thousand ostriches had died to make it. I tried to shut the door, but she shoved a long red leg in a long red boot firmly into the hall.

"Is your mother in?" she boomed in a Voice of Doom.

"Sorry, everyone's out," I mumbled.

"No, I'm not!" shouted Mum, rushing out into the hall.

"Oh... you must be Lady Goodchild..." she said, stopping in her tracks. I think even Mum was a bit taken aback, but she recovered and said, "Do come in. The puppies are all in the kitchen with their parents, so it's perfect timing."

Lady Goodchild swept through the hall, knocking things off shelves with her horrible red umbrella and her enormous bulbous red body and her disgustrous red dead ostriches. The

horribleness of this Dragon gave me hope for a minute. I thought the puppies would be terrified of her, and with a bit of luck they'd bite.

Wrong again.

The faithless puppies, who didn't know any better because they have been brought up to have good manners and be nice to people, swarmed all over the Red Dragon and even Harpo wagged her tail politely.

"Ohhh, they are deeevine, absolutely goooorgeous. Such magnificent fur! And such exquisite markings! Most unusual. Are they as soft as they look? May I pick one up?"

*Now she'll get it*, I thought. No self-respecting puppy would want to be cuddled by this. But no. She picked up – I still can't believe it, even now – she picked up BONZO and he looked absolutely thrilled, his little tail whirling like a windmill. He licked her! Traitor!

"EXACTLY what we've been looking for! Do you know, I'm tempted to buy them all," she boomed. "It seems such a pity to separate the little darlings! And what a handsome father."

Mrs Next-Door simpered and started one of her long drones about how many prizes Lorenzo had won and how it was lucky the puppies had so much of him in them...

"I can see he's a lion," interrupted Lady Dragon, leaving Mrs Next-Door's mouth flapping open and shut like a fish. "And the mother's deeeeevine too! The same sumptuous soft fur! I don't suppose she is for sale as well?"

This was too much for me. I saw the Red Dragon's eyes flashing with greed. I rushed into the kitchen and scooped up an armful of puppies.

"No! She is not! And neither are they! We've changed our minds! The vet says they've got a rare condition!"

"Really?" said Lady Dragon. "What's that?"

"Dog flu!" I shouted. "They've been on Lemsip for weeks! All the rest of us have got it too. The doctor says we're lucky to be alive.

**If you go now you might just escape it!"**



"Dog poo!" shouted Tomato helpfully in the background.

Mum put an arm round my shoulder, but squeezed a lot tighter than you'd have known from the big smile on her face.

"Trixie's devoted to the puppies, of course," she told Lady Dragon. "It's natural in a child her age. But the puppies are as fit as fiddles, and so are we, I can assure you."

"I can understand it. I was the same myself," Lady Dragon said. "I'm happy to wait a couple more weeks while Trixie gets used to the idea. I'll need to make a few preparations before I can take them anyway. But I'm happy to pay you now."

And then she mentioned a very large sum of

money. My jaw dropped, and so did Mum's.

"Are you sure?" said Mum. "That is very generous..."

"I assure you, pups like this are a once-in-a-blue-moon opportunity. It's a very unusual cross, with such a fabulous father..." Mrs Next-Door preened and patted her hair, but I'm sure Lorenzo rolled his eyes. "I'll write you a cheque which you can bank, and I'll call you in a few days to let you know when I'm ready to collect them. Here's my number in case you need to get in touch."

"Well, I must say that is good news. It's lovely they can all stay together, isn't it, Trixie?"

"They're all together NOW!" I shouted. "And this is their home!"

I grabbed Bonzo and raced upstairs, with Tomato running along behind.

"Whassa matter?" he cried.

"Oh, they're going to sell the puppies to that woman," I said. "She's going to take ALL the puppies away!"

At last the penny dropped. "NOOO!" shrieked Tomato. "Howwid wed woman! No!" He hurled himself at me, struck down by grief. I was touched.

"Don't worry, Tom-Tom," I said. "We'll save them somehow."

Tomato looked at me smiling. "Clever Twix," he said.

"That's right," I said.

We looked at each other for a bit. Then I remembered Mum had said the Red Dragon lived in Mandleton. Wasn't that where the science lab was? The one where Chloe said they do animal experiments? The Shame of Bottomley?!

"What are we going to doooo?" I wailed, burying my head in Bonzo's fur.

# Chapter 3

That night, I dreamt I was being kidnapped. I couldn't see my attacker, but I was hauled out of bed and stuffed into a sack. I struggled and fought but I couldn't escape and I could feel myself being dragged along for what seemed like hours.

Then I was pulled out by a pair of pink TROTTERS and found myself face to face with an enormous pig dressed in a chef's hat and apron. Chloe was there too, trussed up like a chicken and terrified.

"This one's ready," said the pig, patting Chloe. "But this one needs fattening up," and he poked me in the ribs.

"Yeah, put it in the pen and feed it up. It'll be ready for Christmas," snorted a pig in dungarees. "Be lovely with some mashed swedes and turnips."

"Don't! You can't eat me! I'm a person!" I shouted.

"They all say that," said the pig, sharpening his knife.

"But I'm a vegetarian!" I squeaked.

"Yum, organic. Makes no difference to me," said the pig. And as he said it he picked up Chloe and chopped off her head.

I woke up screaming, "CHLOE!"

Some dreams stay with you all day and I couldn't stop worrying that this one meant something

bad would happen to Chloe, but when I told Dinah about it at school later that day she said it just meant I was worried about the puppies. Worried that the disgustrous Red Dragon would eat them or something.

So I told Chloe about the dream and she agreed. "This red woman sounds just like Cruella De Vil, that horrible woman who steals the puppies in *101 Dalmatians*," she said.

"Exactly," I said, remembering with a shiver of horror the way she had gone on about their beautiful soft fur. "I'm scared she's going to skin them for a coat or make them into pies."

"Probably both," said Dinah gloomily. "That's why she doesn't want to come and get them yet – so they'll be bigger and fatter by then, with more fur and more meat!"

"Mmmm, lovely! Dumb animal stew and puppy-skin gloves!" Orson swaggered by with a gang of Year Sixes.

And, thanks but no thanks to Orson, that's what gave me my Best Idea Yet. Not that I'd ever let on to him that he'd helped me. "I think your brother's looking for you," I told him wittily.

"Haven't got a brother," said Orson, falling into my tricky trap.

"You mean there's another boy who looks like a dead goat wearing a bin bag in this school? Get that."

Orson lunged at me. Dinah stuck her foot out and he crashed into the Nature Corner where Year Threes put out nice displays of leaves and twigs they've found on the way to school, along with rabbit droppings and bus tickets, that kind of thing. All the little exhibits went flying.

Me and Dinah zoomed off and hid in the toilet.

"Just because he's a bully, you shouldn't bully him back," said Chloe.

"Serves him right," said Dinah.

"Whatever. Now listen to my Big Idea," I said. I could feel the light bulb of wisdom glowing in my brain. "That stuff about 'dumb animals'. That's what most people think, isn't it? That animals don't have lives of their own. They're just there to be cooed over or dragged around or eaten by us horrible humans."

"Well," Chloe considered, "Animal Rights people don't think that."

"Yeah, but they still think animals need protecting. It's still treating them as a lower form of life," I said, getting more excited by the minute. "Look, I think my dream was a message from the Animal Kingdom. The pig was trying to prove that animals are people too, that they don't deserve to be eaten or mistreated any more than the rest of us. But there's more to it than that, more than even Animal Rights people think."

"Go on," Dinah said.

"I'm going to prove to the world that animals are not dumb and they are probably just as clever as we are. MORE clever in fact, because they don't have wars or need all the stupid stuff we need. Like mobiles and mops, and... and... pillows.. and...pop music... and... pencils and diets and dentists and diaries, and..."

"All right, we've got the point," Dinah said. "Or maybe we haven't. What is it?"

"The point is that animals don't go to school like we do, so they don't have a chance to learn anything except smelling lampposts and barking and stuff. So you know what I'm going to do?"

Dinah and Chloe were looking at me in a goldfishy way. They shook their goldfishy heads

from side to side. In fact, they were beginning to look like goldfish who had just met a very sad, wounded, lonely, tragic goldfish. But I carried on.

"I'm going to teach the puppies to read! Then Mum won't be able to sell them. It would be like selling her own children!"

Dinah and Chloe didn't say a word at first. Then Dinah got her breath back. "Look, Trix, don't take this personally," she said, linking arms with me, "but you've gone nuts. You're talking out of your bottom. It's the stress. But Chloe and me can help you through this. That's what friends are for."

"You don't understand," I said. "The only reason animals don't do what we can do is that they are prisoners. Just like women used to be when they weren't allowed to do anything except have babies and cry. If we MAKE THE

EFFORT to teach animals, then they will learn."

Chloe and Dinah were now smiling at me sympathetically, and nodding.

I carried on regardless. "Look, dogs understand simple commands, don't they? Like 'sit' and 'walkies' and 'fetch'? So why shouldn't they learn to *read* words as well? It's only because no one's ever thought of teaching them."

Chloe nodded again and Dinah rolled her eyes.

"I'm sure it's possible," I went on. "You've heard those stories about kids being found in the jungle, brought up by wolves or gorillas. They're not like humans. All they can do is grunt and scratch and stuff. So all animals need is to be brought up like babies are."

**Dinah and Chloe glanced at each other. The glance said Trixie Has Lost Every Single One Of Her Brain Cells And Needs To Go And Lie Down Somewhere Very Extremely Quiet For A Very Extremely Long Time.**

"Wait," I said. "I know I saw something about this on the Internet. I'm sure that someone somewhere has taught a chimp to read. All it takes is dedication."

Dinah said I could try to teach the puppies astrophysics if I really wanted to, but count her out because she had more important things do.

"Like what?" I said, miffed. What was more important than the Greatest Breakthrough in Life On Earth since the dinosaurs got hit by the asteroid?

"Can't tell you," Dinah said.

"What, what?" coaxed Chloe.

"Oh, all right. I'm going to find a way to meet Vera the Vegetarian Vampire."

Looking at Dinah, I could see this wasn't a joke. Now it was my turn to look as if she was mad. Vera the Veggie Vampire is the star of a TV series everybody watches. Dinah's been obsessed with her for a year and spends ages acting it out. She does all the voices, even the weird whine of Wendy Watercress, always boasting about how healthy she is. Dinah's brilliant at it, but it can drive you mad sometimes.

"Dinah, don't be daft. How could you get to meet Vera? She's a mega-star."

"I'm going to persuade her that she needs to talk to real kids, to keep in touch with her audience."

"Well, I think it's a great idea," said Chloe encouragingly, "Look, Trixie, it's not that we really think you're crazy about animals reading—"

"It's not?" squawked Dinah.

"But Dinah's right. We've all got other things to do – like investigate the lab in Mandleton, to see if any evil testing is going on. That's going to be a big task."

"Of course," said Dinah, "we could always do that and help poor Trix out at the same time. We could spy on the Lady Venus Goodchild to find out if she's doing horrible experiments on animals. Might end up being a way of getting the puppies back."

Chloe nodded. "I think there's even a clue in her name. She's trying to sound good; the opposite of Cruella De Vil. Venus, is a Roman Goddess, or is it Greek? Anyway, it's the opposite of devil. And GOODchild is the opposite of cruel."

"That's a bit random," I said.

"Random? Says someone who thinks puppies can act Shakespeare," said Chloe huffily.

"I did NOT say they could act Shakespeare," I

said. "But, come to think of it, why shouldn't they? It's worth a try..."

Dinah and Chloe went off shaking their heads.

I went home and logged on.

I couldn't find any stuff on the web about animals learning to read, but I was convinced that that was just because nobody had ever tried to do it. But finally I found a true story about a bloke who had taught a chimp called Washoe to understand sign language. Washoe learned more than a hundred words! She even managed to produce simple phrases like "more fruit", "gimme tickle" and, best of all, she signed "open food drink" to get someone to open the fridge.

At about the same time as Washoe was learning sign language, two other scientists taught a chimp called Sarah to use plastic shapes to communicate! I found this Very Extremely amazing description:

Sarah eventually managed to produce more complicated sentences like, "If Sarah put red on green, Mary give Sarah chocolate."

I even found a thing on the BBC website about haddocks singing love songs.

**There! I was right! Fish sing, chimps chat, probably puppies COULD act Shakespeare.** Animal Liberation, like Women's Liberation, is Only a Matter of Time. And I, Trixie Tempest, will be a campaigner in this great cause...

I spent the rest of that evening figuring out ways to teach the puppies. Since my two so-called best friends didn't believe in my plan, I decided my best helpmate was going to be Tomato. He was learning to read and could probably give me some tips. I lured him into my room with marshmallows.

"Right, Tomato, we're going to do a secret project but you've got to keep it under your hat."

Tomato zoomed out of the room and came back with his woolly bobble hat, his cowboy hat, his Batman hood and his new baseball cap. "Which one?" he asked.

"Keeping it under your hat's just a grown-up saying, Tom-Tom," I explained. "It means keeping something Very Extremely Secret. If we want the puppies to stay here, we have to teach them to be Very Extremely Clever, so that Mum wants to keep them just as much as we do. But you can't tell Mum what we're doing."

Tomato danced a little jig. He does care about the puppies almost as much as I do really. It's just that his attention span is very short, so if it's a

choice between puppies and pasta, I know which he'd choose.

"Tom-Tom, what are your favourite books?"

He fetched a *Batman* magazine, *The Beano* and a little plastic bath book called *Danny Duck* from his room.

I knew he couldn't read *Batman* or *The Beano*, but just liked the pictures. I asked if he could read

*Danny Duck* and he proudly recited:

*Danny duck is a happy duck.*
*He swims and swims all day.*
*Danny duck is a happy duck.*
*What does Danny say?*
*QUACK QUACK QUACK!*

*Connie cow is a happy cow.*
*She's in her field all day.*
*Connie cow is a happy cow.*
*What does Connie say?*
*MOO MOO MOO!*

I interrupted him at this point. He was about to tell me all about Percy Pig and Barry Beetle and Shiona Sheep.

It flashed across my mind that maybe I wouldn't have the patience for this teaching stuff, but I summoned up the vision of the digustrous Red Dragon, Lady Goodchild, and told Tomato how clever he was.

"How long did it take you to learn to read that book, Tomato?"

But Tomato didn't know.

"Let's see if we can teach it to the puppies. We'll start on Bonzo."

We tempted Bonzo into my room with a juicy Fidoburger.

Tomato held the book open and I pointed to Danny Duck. "Look, Bonzo. DUCK." I said.

Then I pointed to Connie Cow. "Look, Bonzo. COW."

Bonzo looked.

"Now, Bonzo, listen. I'm going to hold up a picture. If I show you a duck, wag your tail, but if I show you a cow, don't wag your tail. OK?"

I held up the duck picture and Bonzo drummed his little tail against the floor.

"Clever boy!" and I gave him half the Fidoburger.

Then I got Tomato to do the same. Except that he pointed to the word DUCK and said "COW". And Bonzo just wagged his tail all the time whichever picture it was.

"Tomato, you're confusing him. Why'd you say cow instead of duck?"

Tomato went redder than ever, which is Very Extremely red indeed, and the truth dawned. He wasn't reading it at all. He just knew it by heart.

I decided to find out more about teaching reading and who best to ask? Mum of course! Here I was, living with a teacher under my very own roof.

"Do you realise Tomato isn't reading a word of that *Danny Duck* book?" I asked her. "He just remembers it. Don't they teach kids anything these days?"

"Of course he isn't reading it yet. He's only

four," said Mum. "All kids start off learning things by heart, like nursery rhymes."

"Did I do that?"

"Hmmm. As I recall, you used to correct me every time I got a word wrong when I read to you..."

"And now you never read to me. You only ever read to Tomato!"

Mum looked stricken. "Would you like me to?"

"Er, yes," I said, because suddenly I really liked the idea of being tucked up warm and cosy with someone reading to me about a giant rabbit. "But Dad does it better." This was true. Dad always used to read putting on all the voices and sometimes adding silly words to make me laugh, while Mum always read as though her life depended on getting to the end of the book and then slamming it shut. "You were always in a hurry."

"Oh dear. Was I? I suppose I always am," said Mum sadly, looking at her watch. "And now I'm late as usual."

"Late for what? It's six thirty in the evening!"

"Parents' meeting." And she was off.

"How do you teach kids to read?" I bellowed at her back.

"With patience!" she screamed back.

# Chapter 4

**Next morning, Dinah and Chloe grabbed me on the way to school.** "Do you know who she is, that Goodchild woman?" Dinah said excitedly.

"A monster," I said.

"Right!" said Dinah. "My mum knows all about her. She's apparently always in the papers, filthy rich, winning awards for this and that. Her family runs Goodchild's clothes business. You're probably wearing something of hers right now."

I shivered and looked myself up and down. I couldn't see anything that looked obviously as if it had once been a puppy, though I was a bit worried about my trainers.

"And Goodchilds make a lot of parka jackets. And you know what THAT means!" said Dinah.

"Erm, not exactly..."

"Parkas have fur collars!"

"But it's fake fur, isn't it? Mostly?" I said hopefully.

"Well, that's what it says on the LABEL... But I looked on the Internet and it says some of these coats have fur made from dogs and cats!"

Help.

"Look, I hate her all right, but we don't know for sure that she makes her stuff out of pets," I wibbled.

"Aha," said Dinah. "But I'm going to find out."

"How?"

"I'm going to ring up Lady Horrible and tell her I've got a big supply of dog and cat fur, is she interested? If she is, we've got her!"

**Dinah is Very Extremely brilliant at doing**

other people's voices – she is bound to be a world-famous actress one day, so if anyone could be a fake Fur Bandit and fool Lady Dragon, she could. But I was still worried.

"It's a great plan, but even if she is an animal murderer, it won't stop my mum selling the puppies to somebody else," I said gloomily. "That's why I've still got to prove they're just as human as we are."

"How's that going?" Chloe asked me. I caught Dinah winking at her.

"Not very well," I said. "I think maybe Bonzo has learning difficulties. But I'm not going to give up yet."

"Maybe you're not showing them something that relates to their lives," Chloe said.

"Are you mocking me?" I said, waiting for another blast of sarky jokes from my so-called friends.

"No, I'm serious," Chloe said. "You could do a book just for animals. Or a magazine would be even better!"

"Yeah," said Dinah, smirking, "with horoscopes for horses, called Horse-o-scopes. And

pin-ups, like 'Stallion of the Month'"

"Yeah," said Chloe, "and Doggy-Treat recipes, and beauty tips like how to style your mane and tail."

"Then if they won't read that, they won't read anything," said Dinah.

"You're just laughing at me," I moaned. "But I'll prove it to you. I know! Let's have an animal talent contest! To find the cleverest pet. Anyone can put their pet in, whatever it is, and there'll be prizes. I bet we'll find one that proves me right."

"Well, it'll be a laugh, if nothing else, I suppose," Dinah said. "All right. But first of all I'm going to catch the Red Dragon and unmask her for the foul animal-exploiter she obviously is. According to my mum, she got rich by getting the work done in places like China and Korea, where they pay low wages. So if I pretend I'm from China, she'll probably talk to me. Trouble is, I don't know how to do the accent."

"What about the Chinese lady in the chippy?" said Chloe. "We could drop in there for chips on the way home from school and get her talking so you can hear her voice."

So that's what we did. Poor old Mrs Chang can't have talked so much in years.

"You're all very chatty today," she said as she doled out three lots of mushy peas and four bags

of chips. (Chloe needed two.) Mrs Chang must have wondered why we asked her what her favourite animal was, whether she had a fur coat and all sorts of other daft stuff about running a business, how many haddocks she sold and all, whatever. We wanted to hear her say as many key words as possible including DOG and CAT and FUR and TRADE and POUNDS.

Chloe and me were halfway down the street, with Dinah lagging behind, when we heard Mrs Chang shout, "Stop thief! They've stolen my battered sausages!"

**We leapt out of our skins and looked round in terror to see Dinah bent double with laughter. Dinah is amazing.** She had only listened to Mrs Chang for a few minutes, and she could already imitate her voice perfectly.

"You nearly choked me!" I spluttered.

"But you are, really, a genius," said Chloe. "How do you DO that?"

Which made Dinah's day.

"OK, so I can do the voice. But what am I going to SAY?" Dinah looked worried.

"Tell her you want to meet her to talk about a business proposition," Chloe said. "Tell her you've got a big supply of... er, materials... at a very attractive price. That's the kind of stuff business people go on about."

"And we could put Tony Scribble on to it!" I suddenly thought. "That reporter from the *Bottomley Gazette* who wrote about my nit farm. You know, the one who looks like a set of rabbit's teeth held together by spots. He could listen in on the meeting and then blow her wicked plans wide open!"

After about six tries, we found a working phone box. We didn't want to be traced by using a mobile or a phone at home. Dinah rang the number the Dragon had left with my mum.

"Hello, can I speak to Lady Goodchild?" she said, in her fab new Chinese accent.

There was a long silence while the butler or

maid or whoever it was, went off to find Dragon Lady. Dinah was all excited now and she was brilliant!

Me and Chloe were straining to hear what Lady Goodchild said, but we couldn't. All we heard was Dinah's bit and it was cool. She said her name was Dinah Yen and that she had a supply of the kind of material that "busybodies" had made very hard to get these days. She was sure someone as successful as Lady G would appreciate what she meant and it was a once-only offer that was too good to miss. Dinah then nodded a lot and wrote down a date. Then she said "Goo-bai" and hung up.

The date was this coming Monday.

"Oh no, that's parents' evening," Chloe groaned. "Couldn't she do it sooner?"

"She's away in Korea," Dinah said. "Don't worry, it's fixed for two hours before the parents' thing. There'll be plenty of time. I gave her the address of that old warehouse of my dad's in Mink Street. Only one problem, of course."

"What???" Chloe and I asked.

"ME, you airheads. How am I supposed to meet her? Do I look like an old Chinese fur-smuggler?"

We had to admit she didn't.

"What have we done?" murmured Chloe tragically. We were now sure that Lady Goodchild was the spider at the centre of an international puppy-slaughter ring. Who knew what might happen if she caught us out?

"Well, she doesn't have to see you, does she?" I said slowly. "I mean, this is a big secret sneaky criminal thingy, isn't it? You could hide in the shadows, tell her it's better she doesn't see your face. Then she won't be able to give you away when she gets tortured by special Animal-Rights agents."

"We don't want to scare her off," Chloe warned.

"All right, don't tell her about the agents. But a secret identity would be OK. Crooks are always doing that in the movies. We'll be hiding in the somewhere in the warehouse. Behind boxes or something."

"OK, I'll do it," Dinah decided. "Just don't run away and leave me if things go wrong."

"We won't," I answered for me and Chloe. But I sounded braver than I felt. In my heart of hearts I thought we could always just not go to the meeting with the Red Dragon. But I didn't want to say so, not yet...

That night, when Mum had got back from work knackered as usual, I badgered her for more information about reading. (I wonder why they say that? Did they used to set badgers on people until they told you what you wanted to know?)

**She reeled out a whole long list about how complicated the process of learning to read is and how it takes some kids ages, and she told me a few bits and pieces about boring reading**

schemes and flash cards, and all sorts of stuff which I could feel going in one ear and straight out the other without pausing to stop in my brain.

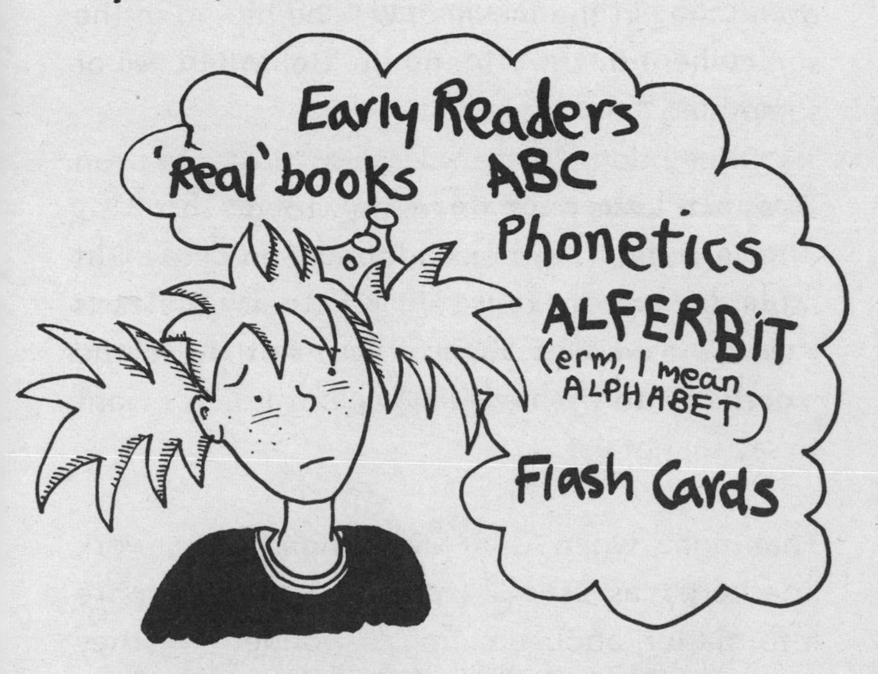


"But what's the really earliest thing? You know, like a toddler might understand?"

Mum frowned. "Well, I suppose the first thing I tried to teach you was to count to ten and to know your colours, but most kids start nursery not knowing those things and it doesn't do them

any harm. You can try to cram too much information into a child when really it should be just making mud pies."

"Why are you a teacher then, if you think kids would do better making mud pies?"

"Someone's got to do it," groaned Mum. "Now, off to bed."

I couldn't sleep for worrying. I kept thinking that animals have the right to be free, like kids do, so why force them into disgustrous schools and stop them from running about sniffing each other's bottoms?

Hmmm. Maybe people should NOT be quite as free as animals...

On the other hand, I had to save the puppies from the Red Dragon, and how else could I do that except by proving they understand stuff as much as a child does?

Eeek.

But the next day I had a whole lot more to worry about.

"Won't we just get the same bunch of losers who turned up to the Amazing Talking Dog show?" Dinah asked.

Me, Dinah and Chloe were sitting on my bed trying to design a poster to advertise The Great Genius Animal Contest which we'd decided to hold on Saturday. You might remember the Talking Dog Show from my first fantastic book, *The Amazing Doggy Yap Star*. It ended in a series of unfortunate events.

"Do you remember Gertrude the curtain-eating goat?" said Dinah.

"Yes, and Humphrey the harpooning hamster. And the ham sandwich getting wedged in your mum's CD player. And the bath full of chicken feathers," I nodded.

"And Orrible Orange Orson dissolving a slug with salt," added Chloe, shivering.

"Euk. Well, anyway, this won't be anything like that," I said. "That was about doing stupid tricks. This is about having real intelligence. And we'll do it outside, in the park. We can use the bandstand as a stage so we can't wreck the place. We're not charging money either – we're just finding the cleverest animal in Bottomley."

"So we can teach it Shakespeare in, erm, just ten days," said Dinah.

**"It was SIGN LANGUAGE the chimpanzees learnt!" I shouted. "I am fed up with you not believing any of this."**

"What about prizes?" said Dinah, deciding to avoid the argument for once.

"How about that horrible orange party dress your auntie gave you? The one that was two sizes too big," I suggested.

"Ohmigod, yes," Dinah gasped, 'it almost fits me now, so I've run out of excuses for not wearing it. If we give it away I can say I just got felt-tip on it accidentally and had to throw it away. Bit of a rubbish prize though, isn't it? And supposing a boy wins? I can't see Dennis or Sumil in that dress."

"Maybe William, though," I considered.

"Yeah," Dinah pondered, "maybe William. But I think the dress is too disgusting for a prize. My sister's got loads of stuff she never wears and loads of books she never reads and CDs she never listens to."

Dinah's Big Sister Dora is not my favourite person, as it happens. She has none of Dinah's wit, wisdom, talent or sense of fun. She is like a head teacher disguised as a teenager. I couldn't imagine her having any stuff a self-respecting kid would want to win, but I said, "Great, and we can buy a fat box of choccies for second prize."

"Who's 'we'?" said Dinah. "I'm broke."

"We'll think of something. First, we'd better do the posters."

Chloe's. OK. Good words.

Rubbish drawing by Dinah.

Here are the posters we made. Mine is the best, as usual. But we decided to use them all for variety.

Dinah scanned them on her mum's fancy computer and we went on printing them until the printer ran out of ink, after which we stuck a message on it saying IT WAS LIKE THIS WHEN WE GOT HERE.

Then we went out to put up the posters, mostly on trees and lampposts, although we persuaded Burly Bert the Demon Barber, Mrs Chang at the chippy and Mr Bunn at the bakery (yes, I know, it's just like Happy Families here in Bottomley) all to put one in their shop windows.

"My boy Shane could bring old Einstein along," chuckled Burly Bert. "Talk about sharp. Opens cans wiv 'is teeth."

*Who's Einstein?* I wondered. I had visions

of an alligator, but it seemed the wrong moment to ask.

Mrs Chang was interested too and started on about a friend's cat who could skateboard. "It's not about party tricks though, it's about finding animals with a really high IQ," said Chloe.

"Oh yes," said Mrs Chang. "IQ. Mine's 156."

"What's IQ?" I asked Chloe on the way out.

"Intelligence Quotient," said Chloe, looking at me in amazement.

"So is 156 high?" I asked.

"Mmm. Genius nearly," said Chloe.

"Then why's she running a chippy?"

"Clever people never earn money. They often do jobs like that," said Chloe dreamily. I bet Chloe's IQ is at least 170.

I was encouraged by Burly Bert and Mrs Chang. I was sure there would be loads of brilliant

genius animals in Bottomley. All we had to do was to find them and soon they could be running the world. I would vote for the Dog Party, no problem. They would definitely be the party to put grass over all the streets. Maybe we'd have to have a few cats involved to bury the poo though.

We had a tough time persuading Mr Drugg, even though Chloe talked to him for ages about liquorice.

"I can't take posters unless you pay me," he said.

"It's only for a few days, till Saturday," I pleaded. "All the other shops have said yes."

**Mr Drugg swivelled his eye.** "All the other shops aren't making their living from a noticeboard," he grumped. "If you pay, that's fine." Then he took a closer look.

"Interesting..." he stroked his knobbly chin. "I may know of just the animal you're looking for."

"Great! Then it might win the Grand Prize on

Saturday," I beamed. And eventually he let us put up the poster for free.

We pinned loads more to lampposts after that and I saw yet another sad poster for a missing cat. It was pinned to a tree and written in red felt-tip, obviously by a kid, and it had gone all runny in the rain. There was a very small blurry photo of the cat, who looked like about a thousand other cats. It made you want to cry.

"The plot thickens..." said Dinah, staring at it. She looked at her watch. "Gotta go. I'll be late."

Late for what? I wondered.

Chloe came back to mine and I moaned about Dinah and how she wasn't taking any of this very seriously. "I don't think she's going to go to the meeting with the Red Dragon," I grumped.

"Well, maybe she shouldn't," said Chloe. "It won't be very safe."

"Safe. All you care about is safe. The puppies aren't safe."

"Well, show me what they can do."

So here's what I did to impress Chloe. I put Bonzo outside my bedroom and hid a juicy Fidoburger under my pillow. Then "Bonzo," I shouted. "There is a juicy Fidoburger under my pillow. Find the Fidoburger."

repeated this experiment three times, each time putting the Fidoburger in a different position.

Each time I told him where it was and each time he went straight to it!

"See? He now understands a whole lot of words."

Chloe was being very quiet and very not excited. Why is it that no one believes in my Great Animal Intelligence Project except me?

Finally she said, "Have you tried to get him to find anything else? Like a book? Or, erm, a cup?"

"No. Why would he want to find a book or a cup? He just wouldn't bother. Like when Warty-Beak tells us to count lorries going past the playground. We don't bother. We just make it all up."

"Ye-e-s," said Chloe doubtfully. "So why not ask him to do it with a ball? He likes balls, doesn't he?"

"All right, if you insist."

It didn't work.

"Er... have you noticed dogs rely on their sense of smell quite a lot?" Chloe asked.

Then the penny dropped. Bonzo could SMELL the Fidoburger. He wasn't listening to what I was saying; he was just following his nose.

**Oh boo.**

"What about sign language? They've taught it to chimps," I said to Chloe. I had a feeling this was something Chloe the Brainiac might know about, and I was right.

"Well, you can sign all the letters of the alphabet and make loads of words and phrases. This is the one for Food:

"The closed right hand goes through the natural motions of placing food in the mouth. This movement is repeated."

"Then you can do phrases – stuff like 'What's your name?' – but I don't think most of them would be that interesting to a dog. And, of course, chimps having fingers. Don't know if you've found any on Bonzo, but most dogs haven't got them."

"Don't YOU start having a go at me," I complained. "It's bad enough getting it from Dinah."

After two minutes of gloom I had another bright idea. "How about colours? Couldn't we prove they understand stuff by signing, 'Go get the red ball'?"

"I don't want to be a wet blanket," said Chloe in her best wet blanket voice, but I don't think dogs can see colours the way we do."

I was shocked. "Can't they? You mean those poor little puppies can't see that nice cosy red blanket I put in their basket?"

"They can see the blanket – I'm just not sure they can see it's red. I remember reading that they mix up red and green, like colourblind people do, but I think they see blue and yellow OK."

"What a shame," I said. "So when Harpo and Lorenzo ran off into the bushes together, they couldn't see all those nice green leaves around them."

"Mmmm," Chloe said slowly. "I don't suppose they were looking, anyway. Really interesting, though, isn't it? I'm definitely going to study science."

"YOU are going to study everything Chloe. You have the brain of a mammoth. Sorry, I don't mean it's fossilised," I added, seeing her hurt expression. "I mean it's GIGANTIC."

"And hairy. With tusks."

"That's much cooler than mine, which is a small wobbly, squidgy thing like a pink jelly."

"What does Dinah's brain look like, d'you think? Or Warty-Beak's?"

"Dinah's is a weird mixture of animal and cyborg," I said. "The animal bit isn't squidgy like mine, but firm – it doesn't wobble, it kind of glides. But then it's got this massive memory card wired into it, with samples of all the voices she can do. Warty-Beak's is all wires and magnets and stuff, very old and out of date, so it keeps sparking and blowing up. There's no nice warm pink bits with any feelings or emotions tucked up inside."

"That's it!" said Chloe. "The feeling bit! That's what we really care about with the puppies. We may not be able to teach them stuff, but we know they can feel! We know they can be happy or frightened..."

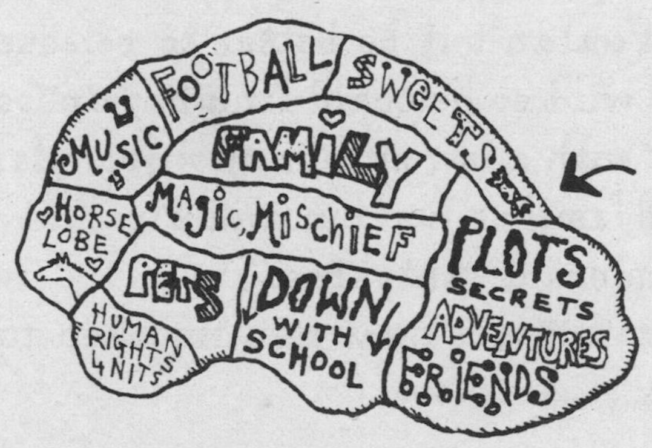


My brain magnified six trillion times

"And we know they can feel hunger and pain," I continued.

"Exactly. So that's how we can persuade people they should be respected," Chloe concluded.

"Chloe, it's not enough; you know that. Everyone knows animals have feelings, but they still treat them like rubbish. I want to prove that they have a right to an education, like we do. I want to prove to the world that animals are people too. If I can't do it, the puppies will be sold and we will have a sad empty house with just me and Mum and Dad and Tomato and Harpo."

"Wish I had all those people in my house," said Chloe sadly, opening her matchbox and looking lovingly at her ant.

**"Chloe, do you think Anty needs some company? Wouldn't it be better to release him into the wild so he could find happiness hanging out with a few million new friends, maybe raise a family – just him and Mrs Anty and 64,000 adorable Antykins?"**

"He wouldn't like it now. He's too used to human beings," said Chloe.

Judging by the way Anty made a beeline, or rather an ant-line, for the open air before Chloe snapped the matchbox shut, I wouldn't have said he was quite as tame as she thought, but I didn't want to hurt her feelings.

"He could use his wider knowledge of the world to help other ants," I suggested.

"You've got it!"

"What?"

"Write an agony column for animals. You've heard of an Agony Aunt? Well, your magazine could have an Agony Ant!"

I sighed. "Yeah, yeah," I said. "But it won't save the puppies."

"How do you know? You're just not thinking it through." I'd never heard Chloe this determined. It was almost scary. "S'pose you do your animals' mag, make it really great, read some bits out at the parents' evening so they all go, 'Ooh, aah, how cute.' Then make a speech right from the heart about how unfair we are to animals, and if we bothered, animals could benefit from all the stuff we benefit from. Then you go, 'And here's the proof – Rover, the dog who can do the *Guardian* crossword, or Benny, the budgie who wins pub quizzes, or whatever hairy brainbox wins the Great Genius Animal Contest.

"Then everybody will go up to your mum and

say, 'How wonderful, good old Trix really cares, what a girl, bet she must have got it from the example you set her. And by the way, how ARE those sweet little puppies you've got?' Well, your mum's not going to want to say, 'Actually, I've flogged them to a dog-murderer' then is she?"

"Chloe," I said. "Be straight with me. Do you really think all this'll happen?"

Chloe squeezed my arm. "Sure, Trixie," she said. "Of course it will."

# Chapter 5

I wasn't giving up on my Animal Education mission. If the puppies couldn't do sign language with their little fluffy paws, and they couldn't learn colours, surely they could learn to count?

Next day I decided to do more research. I couldn't find a lot about dogs counting. The experts seem to think they can tell the difference

between a big pile of stuff and a small pile of stuff. You bet they can. Especially when the stuff is Fidoburgers. The science people who found out this amazingly uninteresting bit of news said they reckoned dogs had learnt it when they were wolves and needed to know which pack of enemies or friends was the biggest. Dogs were wolves 12,000 years ago, so they haven't learned much since. But then, babies wouldn't learn anything if we didn't teach them, would they?

I was determined to teach the puppies to count. I decided it would be my Life's Mission. I would be like that woman who went to live with the apes and made them members of her family. Her own real human family may have found it a bit strange, I suppose. Suppose Dad went off into the jungle for a few months, and brought back a couple of aardvarks and let them scoff Krispy Popsicles with us all in the mornings? Tomato would have trouble with it, that's for sure. And I think I might too.

While I was thinking all this, I became aware of a strange noise behind me. A sort of scuffling, squeaky, squelchy sound.

I looked round to see Tomato scampering out of my room.

"WHAT ARE YOU DOING?" I bellowed.

"Nuffink," he squeaked, or maybe squiggled, if that's what a squeak and a giggle at the same time is. I could hear him galloping away down the stairs like a herd of horses.

I got up to run after him and fell flat on my face. While I was deep in thought about how to make a good future for OUR puppies, **Tomato tied my legs together with string.** But that wasn't all. Hopping out of the door after him, I found myself ankle deep in a large pan of something Very Extremely disgustrous.

I didn't dare look at it. I know the kind of stuff Tomato and his little fiends mix together in pans. One day you'll probably be able to find the recipes for Tomato's famous potions in the Chamber of Horrors or those police museums where they keep stuff about Famous Murderers of History.

I ripped off the string round my ankles and hurtled downstairs three at a time in my saturated socks. Tomato had hidden behind Mum, who was burning some sausages and cursing.

"What on earth is that smell?" she asked. When she saw me, her face changed from a scowl to a look of real horror. "Trixie! What have you been doing? What is that revolting stuff on your feet? Aaaaagh! And all over the floor?"

"ASK HIM!" I yelled, lunging at Tomato.

"Keep away from me, Smelly Bum," squawked Tomato.

My DIY dad had actually finished the posh polished kitchen floor he'd been working on, give or take a few missing bits. I mention this because if he hadn't I wouldn't have slid flapping past my psycho brother and skidded on my socks straight into Mum and the frying pan. Fortunately, I wasn't fried to a chip by the spilling contents of the pan, but the sausages did hit the floor and were swiftly pursued by the yapping puppies, squealing as their noses touched the black and still-sizzling morsels.

Tomato legged it and barricaded himself in his room. But Mum eventually got him to admit the ingredients under a threat of no supper. Tomato's disgustrous potion consisted of: flour, egg, green paint, mustard, washing-up liquid and bread.

He'd kept it in the back garden for a week, which explained the smell. But it could have been worse. At least he hadn't included wee or dog poo.

'"Aren't you going to punish him?" I wailed, after I'd used it as an excuse to lie in the bath for hours.

"Erm, yes. I'm thinking of the appropriate response," said Mum vaguely while she burnt the next lot of sausages. "I'm sorry, Trix, but there aren't any more veggie sausages. Can you make do with just beans on toast?"



That's how it is when you are the oldest. You get tortured by your mad baby brother and then starved. "It's so UNFAIR..." I started, but then the phone rang. It was Dinah.

"I've got something amazing to tell you," she said. "Can I come round?"

"D'you fancy stopping at Mrs Chang's chippie on the way?" I asked her, poking my tongue out at Mum.

Ten minutes later, Dinah was in my bedroom with Mrs Chang's chips. We had to open the window and flap our arms about to get rid of the smell of Tomato's potion.

"Yuck," Dinah said. "I hope terrorists never get hold of the recipe. That'll be it for all of us."

"What's this amazing piece of news?" I said in between chomping chips.

"You know I said I wanted to interview Vera the Vegetarian Vampire for our project?"

"Mmmm."

"She's coming to Bottomley and I'm going to talk to her."

"NO!"

"YES!"

"When?"

"Tomorrow! At the bookshop. She's doing a book signing."

"That will take a long time, won't it? A whole book?" I said doubtfully. My mind was still on sign language.

Dinah looked blank for a moment, then sighed. "I don't mean she's going to read out a whole book in sign language, dummy. I mean she's going to write her signature in copies of books her fans have bought."

"Oh, I didn't know she'd written a book."

"It's an annual to go with the new series, but if it's got 'To Dinah, my friend in the struggle' or something like that, written in her very own writing, it would be my most precious thing I've ever owned ever."

"I wonder what she uses for ink," I pondered. "Beetroot juice? Chlorophyll?"

"Anyway," Dinah said impatiently, "I'm going

to give her this." And Dinah produced a letter she'd written.

Dear Vera,

I am your biggest fan. If you are very busy please skip most of this letter and just read the bit that says VITAL BIT below.

I am doing a school project on saving the animals of Bottomley and I would be very grateful if you could answer this short list of questions.

1. Do you agree that animals are people too?
2. Do you think animals could be taught language like human beings?
3. What do you think of the fur industry?
4. When did you first become a vegetarian?
5. Can I use the Vera the Veggie Vampire design for my animal rights project?
6. How much do you get paid for each episode of Vera?

VITAL BIT: There is another thing, and I know you can help us with it. You can do anything.

We are afraid that there is a lady in Bottomley RIGHT NOW who is kidnapping animals and turning them into fur coats. Lots of pets have disappeared to our certain knowledge and this lady, Venus Goodchild, has just offered to buy my friend's puppies. ALL five of them!! What can she possibly want with five puppies unless she is going to skin them and turn them into fur collars for her horrible coats? Or could she be going to sell them for even MORE money to horrible scientists doing experiments?

Please please can you help save the puppies?

We believe that if animals had a proper education, like children do, that they would be able to learn all sorts of stuff that would be helpful to humanity and also stop people wanting to eat them.

PLEASE PLEASE answer. Either post it back to me (SAE enclosed) or email me the answer to ddv@ddv.co.uk.

Yours faithfully,
Dinah Dare-deville

"You've packed a lot in," I said, a bit overwhelmed.

"Well, how many times do you get a chance to have a real live superhero help out with your schoolwork?" Dinah said. "AND help you track down a gang of heartless villains at the same time?"

I couldn't help agreeing.

So the next day, me and Dinah and Chloe ran out of school as soon as the bell went to get ahead of the queue at Vera's book signing. But even so, it already seemed to stretch for miles from the door of Badger's Books when we arrived, all the way down the High Street and almost to Mrs Chang's.

"I didn't know there were so many Vera fans in Bottomley," I said. "It's just like trying to get to see Jacqueline Wilson or JK Rowling."

"Except they wouldn't all be dressed as vampires and vegetables," said Chloe, eyeing the fans.

"Some of these people are practically grown-ups," I said, as a group of massive shouting boys dressed as Dracula barged past.

"Well, you know, Vera's getting like *Star Wars*, or *Dr Who*. Something for everyone."

And everyone was certainly there. Millions of kids in lettuce and carrot and broccoli costumes.

There was a row of baked beans with a banner saying WE'RE VEGGIES TOO, and a couple of guys advertising the local burger joint in chip suits, which made them look as if they were walking about in golden-brown cardboard coffins, and made it impossible for them to sit down. "It's disgusting," I said. "They're like double-agents, spying for the other side."

"Some people'll do anything for free publicity," Chloe nodded.

A couple of people came as fruit salad, with little plates round their waists like ballet dancers' tutus, and all kinds of stuff stuck all over them – balls painted the colours of grapes, lumps of polystyrene in the shape of pineapple slices, that kind of thing.

It made me quite hungry just looking at them.

"There's so many fans," Chloe said. "It might be difficult to get a chance to give her the letter."

"We'll queue all day if we have to," Dinah said decisively. "She has to sign everybody's book or it's not fair."

We squashed in behind two ladies in banana suits with four tiny Brussels sprouts and an even smaller toddler wearing a box. Dinah raised her eyebrows.

"He's a veggie stock cube," explained one of the bananas proudly. "He made it hisself."

Me and Chloe and Dinah were the odd ones out, in our jeans and trainers. I should have brought Tomato along; he wouldn't even have had to dress up.

Suddenly a fancy stretch limo painted in Vera's colours of carrot orange and lettuce green swooshed up and screeched to a halt outside the book shop. The sunroof opened and Vera emerged through it so everyone could see her.

Dinah's face went all dreamy and she cheered along with the rest of the vegetables.

The Brussels sprouts and the little stock cube started screaming as if Vera was in a boy band. Cameras flashed.

Vera picked up a microphone and began talking about how she'd always dreamed of acting and hoped her success would be an inspiration to a whole new generation. "I'm just

an ordinary girl with an extraordinary talent," she boomed through the loudspeakers on the car roof. "Living proof that you too can be strong and healthy with a good vegetarian diet."

I nudged Dinah. "It hasn't worked for you, has it? You never even look at a vegetable."

"Shhh," said Dinah, jabbing her elbow into me.

Vera was now droning on about diet "...that must of course include plenty of calcium for growing bones. This is especially important for girls..."

"I wasn't expecting this," Chloe whispered. "It's like one of those boring lessons about what's good for you. Food should be fun."

Then Vera went inside the shop to start the book signing. We waited for two hours in the queue, among the tiny vampires and vegetables, just to please Dinah.

"See? It's not just me. This is really big," said Dinah, all excited. "Everyone loves Vera the Veggie Vampire."

We FINALLY got to Vera, but only long enough for her to flash a fake smile at us, and scribble

*To Dinah, love and solidarity, from Vera*

in Dinah's book, then be whisked out of the way so she could move straight on to the adoring mob of Brussels sprouts. **She didn't even notice** the letter Dinah was waving at her, but a woman with an even bigger fake smile, a clipboard and a green top hat with what looked like a leek growing out the top of it, took the letter and stuffed it into a bag.

"I'll make sure Vera sees it, sweetie," she said. Her grinning face looked so much like a joke-shop mask stuck to the top hat that I had to look at her twice to make sure it wasn't.

We got ushered back towards the door. Behind a couple of onions and a few sticks of celery in the queue was a girl I recognised, but I

wasn't sure where from. She glanced over with a sad smile. Then we were outside again.

"She'll never get that letter," Chloe said despondently.

"Then I'll tell her about it myself," Dinah said. She's great like that. When Dinah gets her teeth into something she doesn't let go.

"But we're outside now, in case you hadn't noticed," I pointed out.

"Well, I'll get inside again then," Dinah said. "There's a back entrance down the alley beside the Rose and Crown."

"We're with you," I said.

"We'll get into trouble," Chloe said. "They'll catch us. Her bodyguard's watching that alley."

So we hung about for what seemed like hours. Finally the queue dwindled. Vera'slimo was still outside, with her bored-looking driver sitting in it, reading the paper. Then the big and even more bored-looking bodyguard wandered over from the alley and leaned into the car to talk to him. Dinah was off and down the alley as if she'd been pulled by an elastic band, while me and Chloe panted behind her.

"There she is!" hissed Dinah excitedly. We all ducked behind a wheelie bin to look. Vera was THERE in the alley! And ON HER OWN.

Dinah's eyes went as round as saucers. So did ours. Even Chloe's, which are pretty saucer-like in the first place.

**Vera was leaning against a fire escape, a cigarette in the corner of her mouth. She was pulling something out of a brown paper bag – with the unmistakable logo of a very well-known burger chain on it.**

We scurried along to the next wheelie bin. Vera didn't hear us. We crouched down, not knowing what to do next. Then Dinah stood up. We tried to grab her, but we couldn't.

"That's a beefburger," she said, loud and clear to Vera. "And you're smoking a cigarette. What about your healthy vegetarian lifestyle? You're a cheat."

Chloe and I clutched each other in horror, then stood up very slowly and shuffled behind Dinah, who was trembling – but with fury, not fright.

Vera looked at us and rolled her eyes upwards. "Hell's bells," she said. "No rest for the wicked."

"How can you do this?" Dinah went on. "All those children out there... dressed as vegetables. Because they love you."

Vera blew smoke in the air and sighed. "OK, you got me, darling. But the time comes when you have to face facts. It's like finding out the truth about the Tooth Fairy..."

"What's the truth about the Tooth Fairy?" Chloe said quietly.

"Listen, I'm an actress, kids. I'm just trying to make a living. One day you'll have to do that too."

We just stood staring at her. Even Dinah was speechless.

"Oh God, what am I saying?" Vera suddenly groaned. "Look, don't give me away. Please? I've got a dependent mum and a two-year-old daughter and the dad's a rat—"

"A rat?" Chloe squeaked in horror.

"Not a real rat, love, but he's run out on me and I have to take care of myself. If you tell anybody about this, it'll blow everything. Look, I'll make it worth your while..."

Vera scrambled inside her foliage and brought out a wad of cash. "Take it," she said. "Just keep this quiet, please..."

Our eyes turned from saucers to dinner plates. Dinah drew herself up to her full height. "Keep it," she said. "We won't tell, will we?"

Chloe and I slowly shook our heads, still staring with amazement at the money. For a second, a picture of Gran's smashed cups and saucers, and

my sad dad returning the Wigless Witch's money came into my mind – but it didn't stay long.

"You can't let all those little parsnips and cauliflowers down," Dinah said. "We'll just pretend we never saw this. But you can do us one favour."

"Name it," Vera said.

"Read the letter I gave your assistant – please. My email's written on it. Then let us know if you will help us with the things I've asked."

**"You got it, darling. No probs. I'll do it as soon as we get back to the office. And thanks for this. Want the rest of the burger? It's a bit cold now."**

Dinah wrinkled her nose. "No thanks."

"OK, well – see you around. Bye for now. I'll be in touch." And then she was gone.

"Do you think she'll read my letter?" said Dinah on the way home.

"I doubt it," said Chloe, in her best gloom-of-doom voice. "What a fake."

AT least Dinah got her book signed. But I had a feeling we weren't going to hear any more from Vera.

# Chapter 6

I was wrong. Next morning, Dinah came to school with a face like a sack of spanners.

She'd had an email from Vera.

But even she had to admit it was rubbish.

Dear Dinah,

Thank you so much for your gorgeous letter and fabulous drawing! I was born on February 10th and my star sign is Aquarius. Like many Aquarians I am very romantic and have naturally jet black hair and dreamy green eyes. So, no, I don't wear a wig or use tinted contact lenses! I always had a great love for the stage and went to a special school for extremely talented children, which specialised in dance and drama. Wasn't I lucky not to have to do boring maths?!

My first job was a toothpaste advert (although now I should be doing adverts for fang paste!!) and I never looked back! The highlight of my acting career was being offered the marvellous title role of Vera, in Vera the Vegetarian Vampire! As my true fans, like yourself, will know, Vera is my real name, so obviously the part was destined to be mine!

Soon I will be fulfilling another dream, that of STARTING MY VERY OWN RANGE OF VEGGIE BURGERS. The slogan is "Even carnivores can't resist a Vera Veggie Burger". Do watch out for it, I'm sure you'll be tempted.

I'm afraid I can't answer all your questions in detail. If I replied to all my mail I'd never have time to star in the title role of Vera the Vegetarian Vampire! But I'm *sure* you will find what you're looking for on my website www.veraveggievamp.com.

Keep watching the series. There is a fabulous carrot rebellion *being* plotted for next week!

Lots of love,
Vera

We read it in dismay under the tree in the playground.

"That is awful," said Chloe. "She's said all sorts of stuff you don't care about, like what her stupid star sign is, and she hasn't answered any of your questions. I don't think she even read your letter."

**"And I never sent her a drawing! But it's worse than that," said Dinah. "I already know all this from the last online newsletter,**

which I get because I signed up for the website. And the carrot rebellion happened last month! Obviously the assistant just sends out the same email to everyone and changes it a bit to advertise the series."

"Did you go on the website?" I asked.

"Don't be daft. I'm a fan. I read it every day. There's nothing about any of the stuff I asked on there."

"Yeah, but what did you expect really? We already found out she isn't who she seems, what with smoking and meat guzzling."

"Yeah, she doesn't put that on her website. And now she's probably going to make millions out of Vera's Veggie Burgers," said Chloe in disgust.

"Well, she's no help," said Dinah, tossing the email in the bin. "We'll just have to find another way to fulfil our Noble Mission for Furry Rights and save your puppies too."

That evening in my room I lay on the bed cuddling my beloved Bonzo. I couldn't tell Mum and Dad about what had been going on, but

though they could see I was upset, they hadn't made much effort to be sympathetic.

"Bonzo," I said to him, "why is it that whenever you're unhappy about something, grown-ups always just think you are tired or hungry? And if you try to talk about things, they just tell you to go to sleep? Or eat up your dinner?"

Bonzo looked at me wisely as though he agreed with every word, which I think he did. I expect Harpo does just the same kind of nagging with him. "Wag your tail politely" and "You haven't sniffed a lamppost all day" etc.

My Big Idea of educating the puppies had not, so far, been a Very Extremely big success. But at least it's made me sure of what I will do in the future. I'm going to be a teacher! Mainly of animals, but some kids too – there's not much difference. Then I could make school FUN and there'd be no more Warty-Beaks.

To try to take my mind off my troubles, I started work on my magazine, but Bonzo didn't even look at the pictures when I showed him. This is odd because pets are suppose to be interested when they see other animals on TV. Is it possible my drawings are not very lifelike?

Eventually I wrote this heartfelt and Very Extremely touching letter to the Agony Ant.

Dear Agony Ant,
We are five puppies from a close family. We live with our mum Harpo, and our dad

Lorenzo lives next door. We look after three humans – a man, a lady, a Very Extremely nice kind thoughtful girl and a small round red loud thing that might be something from another planet. The lady who we look after wants us to leave and says she will get money for us. We will be split up and have to go to different HOMES!

Is this legal? Is it FAIR?

We know we are breaking animal rules by showing we can write, but a spaniel down the road told us about your magazine, so we think it is allowed. Also, everyone is out so we got to have a go on the computer.

Yours truly,
Marigold, Eric, Fattypuff,
Gertrude and Bonzo.

I showed it to Bonzo and he nodded his head wisely.

"Shall I write a letter back to you from Anty?"

Bonzo yawned, in what I'm sure was agreement.

Dear Marigold, Eric, Fattypuff, Gertrude and Bonzo,

What a truly tragic tail! And a very sad tale too, if I may say so. It is so Very Extremely peculiar, do you not think, that humans think they can do what they like with animals? Research proves that parting puppies from their mothers means that the pups cannot grow into healthy adult dogs. They lose all sense of responsibility and often bite small children or exhibit other forms of criminal behaviour.

Resist this move if you possibly can. Tell this lady that she can no longer live in your house if she continues with talking rubbish.

Ask her, how would SHE like to be sold?

Please let me know how you get on.

Sincerely,

Anty the Agony Ant

I dreamt all night about a tiger who asked me to visit his castle. *How nice*, I thought. *He is treating me like a fellow tiger*. But when we got to his castle there were rugs made out of people, and people's heads stuck on the wall. I screamed.

"Don't you like them?" asked the tiger. "I shot them myself. This one's from Bottomley." And as we got closer, I could see it was MY head! Then he pounced!

I woke up yelling with my mouth full of tiger fur and a loud ringing in my ears.

The fur turned out to be Bonzo's ear. He has taken over Harpo's old habit of sleeping on my head.

Even by break-time, I was still trying to get dog hair out of my mouth, while Dinah and Chloe stood laughing heartlessly at me.

"It's all very well fighting for Furry Rights," Dinah said, "but you don't have to get in the mood by eating the stuff."

"Ha ha," I said. Or rather, "Plfwaar, plfwaaar."

We gradually realised the tall, sad-looking girl

with the enormous braces was hovering about, looking as if she wanted to talk. Suddenly a little something went PING! in my brain. Of course! She was the girl who'd I'd seen waiting in the queue to see Vera, on our way out.

"Shall I come back later?" she said, as I spluttered at her.

"No, it's OK," Dinah said. "She's just choking on her own dog hairs. We might have to take her to the vet for a dose of paraffin or something. It's nothing to worry about. What's your name?"

"Jolene. I saw you at the Veggie Vampire thing yesterday."

"Good, wasn't it?" Dinah said, not very convincingly.

"Well... I don't know. I don't think Vera takes it seriously enough," Jolene said.

"Hmm," said Chloe. "You might be right there."

"You know that letter you left for her?" Jolene said. "The woman you gave it to didn't even bother to take care of it. It dropped out of her bag on to the floor after you went, so I picked it up."

Dinah looked puzzled. "But she must have got it. She sent me a reply. Well, sort of."

"She did," Jolene said. "I made sure the woman took care of it. She was embarrassed in front of all Vera's fans, so she did."

"Thanks very much," said Dinah.

"But I'm afraid..."

"What?"

"I read it first," Jolene said nervously. "I shouldn't have, but I couldn't help it."

Dinah shrugged, but if she was a bit miffed she couldn't complain. Jolene had tried to help. "S'all right," she said.

"And I thought there was something you

ought to know about that woman you mentioned in it. Venus Goodchild."

"What???" we all said at once.

We were all interested now. I forgot about the dog hairs.

"My mum runs the bookshop at Mandleton," Jolene explained. "Lady Venus Goodchild works at that science place there. She gets driven to it in a posh car every day. I was helping Mum there once when she bought some stuff in the shop. She said she was working on an amazing scientific experiment nobody really understands yet and she was looking for dog parts, or something like that. I was shocked she was so open about it."

"That proves it!" Dinah squealed. "She steals animals and experiments on them in that horrible place!"

"I've never heard any screams or howls or anything," Jolene said.

"Well, there wouldn't be, would there?" I said. "It'd be all soundproofed, so nobody got suspicious and the Animal Rights people wouldn't go and camp outside."

"We have to stop her before it's too late, and the puppies all end up being chain-smokers with eight legs that glow in the dark," Chloe said. "No wonder she wanted to meet Dinah to talk about a deal. She must be looking for animals all the time."

Jolene looked curious. "What do you mean?" she asked.

"We've laid a trap for the Dragonous Lady G," I told her. "She thinks she's going to meet a crooked animal-trader to buy cheap fur. We're going to record it and then get it printed in the papers.

"That's wonderful!" Jolene said, clapping her hands. "Can I help?"

"The more the merrier," Dinah said. "We're all scared about it, to be honest."

"Then count me in," said Jolene. "Don't be scared! I'll bring Melchior. And George. They'll protect us!"

"Who's Melchior? And George?"

"My dad," said Jolene, pulling a photo from her pocket. "And his dog. He's my best favourite person in the world. He doesn't live with us, but

one day I'm going to live with him, because when I'm twelve I'll be able to choose."

When she showed us the photo I thought, yeah, we can do this.

You could tell Melchior was huge, because Jolene is tall and she only came up to about his waist in the photo. He looked Very Extremely strong, too. The dog was a little cute wiry thing. I didn't think he'd be much help. But Melchior was the business.

"Is he a weight lifter?" whistled Chloe.

"No. He's a hairdresser," said Jolene.

Dinah looked uncertain.

"But he used to be a bouncer. He's very fit. And George can stand on his hind legs and shake paws. We rescued him from a circus," she added proudly.

"What's a bouncer?" I asked.

"Someone who guards nightclubs and throws out troublemakers," said Chloe scornfully.

"He looks like just the man we need."

So we decided to go ahead with it, even though Dinah was dead nervous. After all, she had the main role.

The Great Furry Rights Fight was well and truly on.

I wasn't sure I could face the Week From Hell to come. The Great Genius Animal Contest was tomorrow. And we didn't even know if anyone was going to turn up. Then on Monday it was parents' evening with our great Furry Rights Appeal, and the Big Scary Confrontation with the Red Dragon. Which might not even work, which meant we'd all end up kidnapped AND I'd lose all the puppies. Talk about stress or what?

"Maybe I'll just have to run away from home with Harpo and the pups," I said to Tomato that evening. I made myself feel quite sad thinking of Mum and Dad looking for me, but I felt sadder when I thought how easy it would be to find me.

**Runaway children may be able to escape on their own, but how could I stuff a huge fat pooch and five puppies up my jumper? Hiding would be impossible.** But Tomato took the idea seriously.

"We could go live with Granny Clump and eat choccies all day," he said.

"She wouldn't give you choccies every day if you lived there Tom-Tom." Still, I wondered.

Maybe we could go to Granny's – she's always saying she doesn't see enough of us.

That night, the night before the Animal IQ contest, I dreamt about the tiger again. This time it was asking me to tea. "Not if you're going to put me in a sandwich," I said. And it laughed a huge roar and I fell out of bed.

I wonder if I need to see a psychiatrist.

I arranged to meet Dinah first thing next day to raid her sister Dora's room for competition prizes for the Great Genius Animal Contest. We couldn't have left it any later if we'd tried. The competition was in the park that afternoon. Would Dreary Dora sink everything?

"It's OK," said Dinah. "She'll be out all day doing her Duke of Edinburgh award."

That is typical of Dora. If she's not studying something, she's doing something hearty up a mountain. If she's not climbing mountains, she's nagging Dinah about something. It makes me grateful for Tomato.

But nicking the prizes from Dora's room was not as easy as I'd hoped. First, Dora's room was absolutely disgustrous – there wasn't even a speck of dust anywhere, or chewing gum, or sweety wrappers, never mind an old sock mountain. Everything was folded and arranged in neat rows or stuck away in drawers.

"Doesn't she have any piles of stuff? It's all so tidy that she'll notice if anything goes missing," I said.

But we'd left it too late for an alternative. We

took two CDs ("She never listens to anything except classical stuff. She hasn't even opened these," said Dinah merrily), an unopened Barbie Princess set, four old books ("She won't want these any more; they're for babies"), a brand new set of forty art pastels ("She never does any drawing") and a pair of really flashy red high-heeled shoes that looked like something the Dragon Lady would have.

"Well, she'll obviously never wear those," said Dinah as we shoved it all into a cardboard box.

I felt rubbish about taking the stuff, even if it was from Dreary Dora. "Isn't this stealing?" I asked Dinah.

"Nah. If it's a member of your own family, it's um, borrowing," said Dinah, looking ever so slightly worried. "No, let's call it recycling." She grinned.

It all took longer than we thought so, armed with our loot and worried by the thought of Chloe having to hold back the hordes of eager pet owners, we ran towards the park.

"Maybe no one will turn up and we can just return all Dora's stuff," I said, half hoping it would be true.

It was not. We heard the animals long before we saw them. And the closer we got, the louder the hullaballoo became. There was barking, squeaking, clucking, neighing, snorting and something that sounded very like trumpeting.

"Ohmigod, I hope nobody's brought an elephant," I said.

"We should have put a maximum size limit," said Dinah. "And what's that roaring sound?"

We turned into the park really scared about

what we might see. Maybe some joker from the zoo had bought a coach load of tigers. In fact, there were more animals in the park than even I had expected. Loads of kids had brought their pets along and their pets were just thrilled to pieces to have so many chums to play with.

The roaring turned out to be a dog who looked like a Rottweiler crossed with a rhino. "Don' be scared, ov 'er," said a small spiky boy in clothes so much too big for him that he did look scarily as if parts of him had been eaten. "Daisy's really friendly. Loves kids."

"For a snack? Or her main meal?" said Dinah.

DOGS MUST BE KEPT ON LEADS, THIS IS A CHILDRENS PLAY AREA said a big sign, but no one paid any attention to it. I could see why. After all, if three goats, a cow (yes, a cow) two horses and four pigs could wander about, then why not let the dogs off the lead too?

Mrs Chang's daughter Mae was there with a bird cage, but the birds in it were either very exotically tiny or had flown away. Burly Bert's son Shane was there with a tortoise. I barely had time to wonder if it was Einstein (do tortoises have teeth?) because Chloe was running towards us, scarlet with indignation.

"Where've you been? You never said the whole TOWN would turn up," she fumed, as though it was all my fault. Which I s'pose it was.

**Dinah sprang into action, threw the box full of Dora's loot to the ground and jumped up on a nearby park bench.** "Welcome to the Great Genius Animal Contest!" she yelled. How wonderful to see so many of you here! May I introduce the judges! Trixie Tempest, well-known animal lover and fighter for Furry Rights, Chloe

Caution, who has a pet ant, and myself, Dinah Dare-deVille, horsewoman and animal lover. We are determined to show the world that animals are people too."

This was met with a chorus of jeers and cheers, and an old bloke with two cows (who didn't

seem fazed that all the other entrants were either children or animals about a millionth the size of his) muttered, "People are animals, that's for sure."

Dinah ploughed on, asking the contestants to form an orderly queue. "We'll do it in alphabetical order," she said.

"I'll be first then," said a long thin boy with a long thin rabbit.

"Rabbits begin with R, don't they?" said Dinah, puzzled.

The boy blushed. "Her name's Abba."

"No, no, we have to do it by species. We don't know all the animals' names, you see," she added kindly because the boy looked on the verge of tears.

The contest was not exactly a huge success.

I was hoping someone would produce an aardvark, as I was thinking it would be Very

Extremely interesting to meet one in real life. Or better still, an ape doing sign language. But the first contestant was an ant.

Its owner, a small girl dressed in what looked exactly like a sack, claimed it could tell the time.

"Whassa time?" she bellowed at it. The ant nibbled a leaf. "See?" shouted Small Sack. "'E's nibbled three bites an' it's three o'clock."

The ant was booed off and the Sack stumbled away cursing, saying she had bought it up from an egg and this was all the thanks she got.

Chloe was pulling at my sleeve. "Anty can walk the tightrope," she whispered.

'"It's not about tricks," I reminded her. "It's about IQ."

"You have to be very clever to walk a tightrope," said Chloe.

"Look, you're a judge. You can't enter as well."

Chloe looked hurt, but I stood firm.

Next was a badger, who was hauled on to the bandstand by a weasely boy of about fifteen. I thought keeping badgers as pets was illegal, and the badger obviously agreed as it immediately made a run for freedom. But it was headed the wrong way! I heard a horrible squealing of tyres and I was all for calling off the whole show, but Dinah promised me she could see badgerkins skipping happily down the High Street with his 'owner' in hot pursuit. There was a car swerved on to the pavement, but nobody appeared to be hurt. So we ploughed on.

The next category was cats. We zipped through them really fast because all they did was sit about yawning. Until we came to Fenella, a Persian fluff ball who was a whizz at counting according to her owner, a small girl in a red velvet dress and patent leather shoes, who obviously thought this was a party.

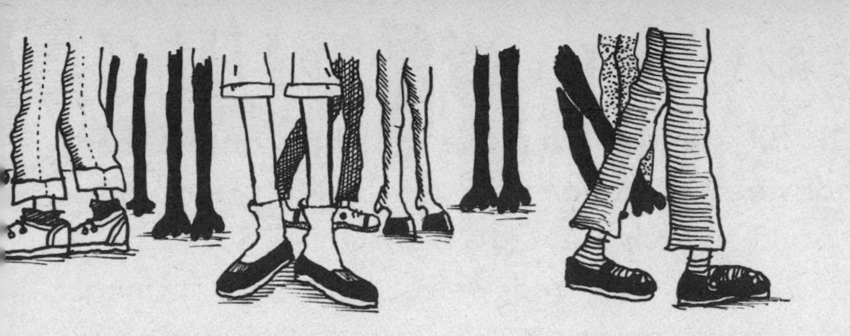

The little girl held up one finger and the cat said, "miaou" (or however you spell cat words).

Then she held up two fingers and the cat said, "Miaou, miaou."

Then she held up five fingers and the cat said, "Miaou, miaou, miaou, miaou..." and then there was a long pause. I swear it, even the goats and pigs shut up.

Then... "Miaou."

The silence turned into a huge cheer.

"She's cheating!" shouted a boy with a very sad-looking ginger cat. "She's pinchin' it!" And she was.

Chloe whispered we should report her to the RSPCA but Fenella looked so fat and happy I let it go.

I bet you'd like to know what the cows did, but unfortunately we never found out. Well, there was one thing they did a lot of, which after

a bit almost everyone at the contest had obviously trodden in, but we didn't think that could be their claim to a high IQ.

Just as the red velvet girl was lisping, "Where'th my prithe?" a distinctly different noise mingled with the mooing, snorting, barking and caterwauling. It was the outraged shouting of four ginormous police officers and one very angry park keeper, all of whom were walking Very Extremely fast towards us. The park keeper's arms were waving about like an octopus in a gale.

"This is a public park! Can't you see the notice?! All dogs to be kept on leads! Remove these animals immediately! Who's in charge here?"

"Doesn't say you can't bring in a cow," said the old bloke, but he was the only one who stayed around to talk. There was

a flurry of paws, claws, hooves, tails, fur and beaks, and suddenly it was just us and some chicken feathers.

"Run!" shouted Dinah.

And we did.

It wasn't till we got back to mine that we realised we'd left Dora's box of stuff in the park.

"We can't go back," said Chloe. "They'll arrest us. What a disaster." For once Chloe's gloom suited the occasion. Nobody said anything for a bit.

"Sorry, Trix," Dinah said, "but I don't think we really proved that Bottomley's full of animal brainiacs just waiting for the chance to be discovered. We found out how stupid a lot of their owners are, but we could have worked that out without going to all this trouble,

or me getting it in the neck from my boring sister tomorrow either."

"OK, OK," I said grumpily. "But it only proves their owners don't understand them, getting them to do all those daft tricks. It's not the animals' fault."

"Well, what could the cow have done that was clever?" Dinah demanded to know.

"Wear a nappy," Chloe murmured. "Learn to drive a milk float."

But we didn't have time to blame each other. The next Big Stress was nearly upon us. Dinah's meeting with the Red Dragon, disguised as the evil animal fur dealer.

We borrowed my mum's best black suit and Dinah's mum's patent leather high heels. Dinah's mum collects shoes, so we were pretty sure she wouldn't miss a pair for one day.

"And there's a Very Extremely grand pair of designer shades that she keeps in her holiday drawer," said Dinah.

I found a massive wide-brimmed black hat that my dad sometimes wears to football matches, when he wants to make himself look like an Italian football manager. People standing behind him tend not to find this idea so much fun.

Once she had all this clobber on,

Dinah looked absolutely amazing. About thirty-five. And if she was mainly going to be a mysterious figure in the shadows, the whole scary scam looked as if it just might work.

"You'll have to wear some lippy too. In case you can't stop her getting up close." I said.

We fixed it for Jolene and her Big Dad to be waiting at the warehouse on Monday. I borrowed my dad's video camera and my mum's digital camera. We were as ready as we could be. But even though we were going to have Jolene and Melchior with us, I was scared stiff of the Red Dragon. And I wasn't much looking forward to parents' evening either. My magazine had turned out OK. I was quite proud of it in fact, but I hadn't taught a single puppy to read a single word and I hadn't found any animal geniuses. My head was a jumble of puppies and red giants.

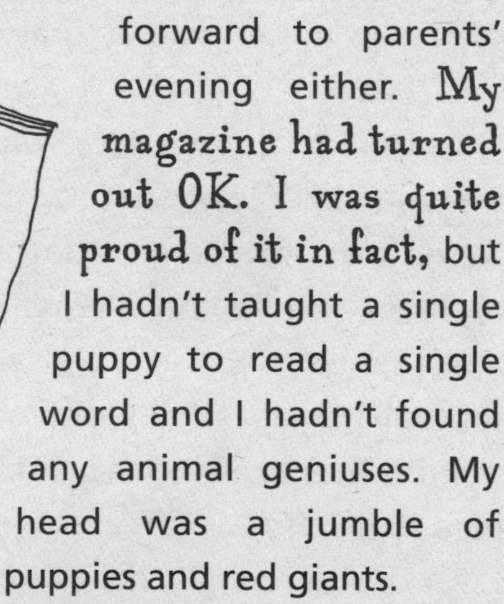

That night, to get myself to sleep, I tried rehearsing my speech for the parents' evening and I finally drifted off with Bonzo snoring gently in my ear.

"Oh, Bonzo," I remember muttering. "How much longer will I hear your sweet soft snore?"

# Chapter 7

The Big Day.

We spent all day at school fixing up the display for parents' evening. All the projects were laid out on two big trestle tables. Ours looked OK, with my magazine, which was ten whole pages in full colour, Dinah's Animal Rights posters with lots of heartbreaking stuff about battery chickens, and Chloe's very careful Insects-of-Bottomley survey. With a

stroke of Chloe-like genius, she had attached it to the paws of a very cute teddy bear, so it looked like he was reading it.

"I wanted to do it being read by an ant, since they are going to take over the world and there are far more of them in Bottomley than people," she explained to Warty-Beak. "But people think teddies are cute, so I am trying to make the project appealing to the masses."

Warty scratched his baldy head. It is rare that

he is lost for words, but Chloe's giant brain quite often has that effect on adults.

Dennis and Sumil had expanded their Lego adventure playground by adding some of the attractions of the town of Bottomley to it. They'd included Chang's Chippy, a pool table and a swimming pool which they'd filled with real water. Unfortunately, they couldn't find any Lego swimming figures, so it was full of astronauts. But it looked great. It was the most work I'd ever seen them do and only goes to prove that if you can get kids interested they will work hard.

We raced for the loos the moment the bell rang and stuffed Dinah into Mum's suit. Clutching the cameras, we galloped over the road to the old warehouse.

As we turned the corner of Mink Street, I could swear my trainers screeched like racing-car tyres. We stopped dead. An enormous man was barring the way in.

*The Dragon's got here first with her minders,* I thought. My insides turned to jelly.

Chloe squeaked a tragic little squeak as though a great boot had squashed her flat.

But then the big man smiled. "Hi, girls, you must be Jolene's friends. I'm her dad, Melchior," he said, holding his has hand out to shake ours. "I thought it might be an idea to bring some back-up," he added, pointing to a small wiry mongrel with pointy ears which he had on a lead.

I recognised the dog from the photo Jolene had shown us. I still didn't think it looked as if it would be all that good in a fight, but it was very pleased to see us.

"He's called George," Melchior explained. "Say hello, George." George sprang up on his back legs and waved his front paws in the air. We all clapped.

"Time's flying," Jolene said, scurrying up to join us. "Hadn't we better get on with it?"

Dinah waited on the corner of the street. We had to be sure Lady Goodchild arrived alone.

Me and Chloe and Jolene and Melchior tiptoed inside. It was dim and scary. All the old stuff stored in there threw strange shadows, but there was enough light for the video camera to get a picture. We hid ourselves behind some boxes while Dinah stood just inside the door, ready to back into the shadowy interior. She was shaking. I wondered what we had let ourselves in for.

We waited for ten minutes, and every one of those minutes seemed like a day. You know how it is, with time. When you are bored in a maths lesson it mopes along like a snail with

the flu, and when you're having the time of your life it's as whizzy as a greyhound. When you are Very Extremely anxious it goes slowest of all.

Finally we heard a purposeful click clack of high heels and there stood the Red Dragon, silhouetted in the doorway, looking even taller and wider and scarier than I remembered.

"Mrs Yen?" she called.

"Lady Goodchild?" came a voice from the shadows. Dinah sounded perfect. What a star.

"That's correct," Lady Goodchild said. "Shall we talk?"

"Forgive me staying concealed," Dinah said. "It's better for both of us."

"How does she do know what to say?" I whispered to Chloe.

"I wrote her a script," she whispered back. "People in books go on at each other like this all the time."

"Ssssh," hissed Jolene, her hand over the microphone on the video camera. "It'll sound like a fix if you keep talking like that."

"I understand," Lady Goodchild was saying to the shadowy Dinah. "So what's your proposition?"

Dinah told her she knew a major supplier of "felines and canines". I was well impressed. She meant cats and dogs.

Lady Goodchild seemed Very Extremely interested. I was surprised she was talking so loud. I knew it would record really well.

"So you have a supply of canines and felines here in Bottomley? Ready to collect?"

"Yes and I can supply a great deal more."

"Where are you storing them?"

"Mandleton," Dinah said. "A secure address. Forgive me if I do not share it with you until the arrangements are complete."

"And your price?" smiled Lady G. "Competitive, I assume?"

"Naturally," Dinah said. "There's no profit in it if you pamper the animals."

"You've come alone, of course?" said Lady Goodchild, peering round. I felt as if her horrible green eyes were boring through the boxes we were hiding behind.

"Of course," said Dinah.

"That was careless..." Lady G paused, then called out: "Gentlemen!" Figures sprouted from the darkness as if by magic.

"MELCHIOR!" I screamed.

"Er, there's rather a lot of them," protested Melchior, not moving. "And I hate to say this, but they look like cops to me."

Me and Chloe tried to run out between their legs but they grabbed us. There was a sickening crunch. **Help? Was it Chloe's neck snapping? Had my nightmare come true? No. Chloe had dropped Mum's camera under the cop's enormous feet.**

"Go easy, Robbie," Melchior said. "They're only a bunch of kids."

"Oh hello, Melchior," the leading policeman said. "Didn't recognise you without a pair of scissors in your hand."

"You coming in to the salon soon? I still don't think that hairstyle goes with your helmet."

"You're probably right. Let's try something different next time."

"I hate to interrupt this," Lady Goodchild said,

"but would you mind getting on with arresting that woman..." (pointing to the elusive black-clad figure of Dinah) "...who's obviously an unscrupulous animal-smuggler?"

"Not exactly, Robbie," Melchior said to the policeman. "She goes to the same school as my daughter Jolene."

Dinah stopped skulking in the shadows and came out, pulling off the shades and hat, revealing that the lippy had smudged across her face, making her look like a circus clown. Kicking off her mum's high heels, she certainly didn't look like an unscrupulous animal-smuggler – more like somebody who'd turned up late and rather cross for a bad school play rehearsal.

"You've got it all wrong," Dinah said defiantly to the

policeman. "It's HER you want!" (pointing at the Red Dragon). "She murders animals for experiments and sells them for coats when she's finished with them."

"That's right!" I squeaked, trying to wriggle free of a policeman's grip on my shoulder. "She's an Animal Assassin! A Puppy Murderer!"

Lady Goodchild took a long look at me. I was trembling in my trainers.

She looked. And looked. And then smiled.

"I know who you are too," she said to me quietly. "You're the little girl who didn't want to sell her puppies."

Something had happened to Lady Goodchild. She wasn't looking angry or mocking or even horrible any more. She looked kind. Her eyes twinkled. She turned to the policeman. "PC Roberts, I owe you an apology.

Well, perhaps we all do. There's been a bit of a misunderstanding."

Lady G gave Dinah a funny, sideways look. It seemed a little bit cross, but a little bit impressed too. "I'm sure we'll all be seeing you on TV soon, my dear," she said. "That was a remarkable performance."

PC Roberts was beginning to look rather impatient. "If no crime has been committed, we haven't got all night, your ladyship," he told her. "The pensioners at the Rose and Crown can get seriously out of order after dark, and the skateboarding in Tesco's car park has become a major policing problem."

Melchior laughed uproariously, then stopped when PC Roberts caught his eye.

"I quite understand, officer," Lady G said, then turned to us. "Correct me if I'm wrong, but my guess is that you thought I didn't want your puppies for pets, but for experiments, or for the

fur trade, or both. By pretending to be traders yourselves, you got me here to trap me into admitting it. What you don't know is that I detest the exploitation of animals. So, thanks to your very convincing performance, I invited the police here in order to trap YOU."

"You m-mean you had no idea about it? But what about that clothing firm called Goodchild's?" stuttered Chloe.

"That's the family firm," Lady G agreed. "But I have nothing to do with it. I'm a scientist."

"Yes! That's right!" put in Jolene. "She works at the laboratory at Mandleton and does horrible experiments on puppies!"

Lady Goodchild laughed.

"Sweetheart, Mandleton's a physics laboratory. We're looking for something called the Higgs boson. It's nothing to do with animals."

"What about the Dog Parts?" said Jolene, accusingly.

For a moment, we thought we had her. Then Lady G laughed. "Not Dog Parts! *God* Particle. The Higgs boson is known as the God Particle!"

Everyone in the room, except Chloe, looked blank, then laughed. And Jolene blushed.

I looked at my watch. It was seven twenty-five.

"We're missing parents evening!" I wailed. "We're supposed to do a thing about Furry Rights and we were going to show all of Bottomley how we'd exposed you!"

"I'm sorry I let you down. You're very brave girls," said Lady G, smiling. And, I find it hard to admit this, but she didn't look anything like a hungry crocodile at all. She looked rather nice. Which only goes to prove that beauty is in the eye of the beholder. "Haven't you got something else to show them?"

"We've got a magazine for animals by animals. And a poster and an insect survey," I admitted. "We were also going to have a thing showing that animals are as clever as humans... but that didn't quite work out either."

"You have my sympathy," Lady Goodchild said. "Things don't always turn out as you want in life – or in science either. But what happens instead can sometimes be almost as good."

Dinah and Chloe and Jolene and I charged off to the parents' evening, leaving Lady Goodchild apologising to the policemen and Melchior offering them all free haircuts to help put things right.

# Chapter 8

**Warty-Beak threw us a filthy look when we finally showed up at school.** But not as filthy as the one Mum threw us when she saw us squeezing into our chairs on stage. *Why does she look so deadly?* I thought. *Ah. She's recognised her best suit. On Dinah. Whoops...*

Warty hissed at me. "We've had to change the whole running order because of your lateness. You go on last. Sit up straight!"

Dennis and Sumil were just finishing their presentation, which was a plea for the Hoodies of Bottomley in rap form. Dennis was reciting the words, while Sumil bounced a football in the air on his knee and his toe in time to it.

"So next time you see a gang of kids in hoodies wiv nuffink to do / Show 'em dat you care about 'em, dey is yuman too!/ Give 'em a yoof centre to burn off all de energy! / Give 'em an adventure playground to destroy fings harmlessly!"

The rows of parents and teachers all laughed nervously.

"Hug a hoodie!" finished Dennis and Sumil together as they shuffled off to a big round of applause from the kids.

Sylvie and Marilyn did a thing about traffic flow in Bottomley, with a lot of graphs and diagrams projected off Marilyn's laptop. Sometimes these came out upside down. but since Sylvie and Marilyn spoke very quietly and the subject was very boring, nobody knew what the graphs meant anyway, whichever way up they were. One of the visuals was a little blue square (a car) going down the High Street, sometimes getting stuck because a little yellow oblong (Mr Arkwright's bus) was coming the other way. Occasionally a very exciting thing happened, which was a little red circle on a stick

(the lollipop lady) stopping the traffic for a whole minute. At the end, everyone who hadn't gone to sleep clapped politely.

Dennis and Sumil and a crowd of other boys at the back encouragingly shouted, "Keep it real!" and made hip-hop gestures, and Sylvie and Marilyn looked quite pleased.

Then me and Dinah and Chloe stumbled on.

"This is about the animals of Bottomley and how they deserve a better deal," I mumbled.

"We were going to prove to you that here in Bottomley an illegal animal trade goes on, run by respected posh members of the community!" Dinah shouted enthusiastically. I frowned at her. "But it turned out not to be true..." she tailed off.

There was a mixture of sympathetic groans and sighs of relief from the audience.

"We were also going to show you some amazing animals that can do things proving they are just as clever as people!" Dinah announced, her tone defiant again.

"But that... er... isn't quite ready yet," Chloe said.

There was another sympathetic groan and one cry of, "Shame!"

"But it IS happening in other countries around the world and we can help stop it!" said Dinah bravely. "Because we believe Animals Are People Too and have as much right to a decent life as anyone else."

**"So, erm, we've made a magazine that you can see on the display table," I struggled on.** "Because we believe that Animals are Not Dumb and one day they will have rights just like us, including a right to an education. And then they will enjoy our magazine..."

By now the whole audience had got the giggles.

"Will they be allowed to vote?" shouted somebody in the front row.

"What about a pet's National Health Service?" said someone else. "Will vets be free?"

Just then a strange buzz went round the room and people started craning their necks to look at something. Warty-Beak and Mrs Hedake got up, ready for action.

Dinah and Chloe and I realised then that we weren't the only ones on the stage. We'd been joined by Melchior's dog, George.

"That dog shouln't be in here!" Warty-Beak shouted.

"Freedom!" shouted Dennis and Sumil and the hip-hop crew at the back.

Warty-Beak and Hedake began to advance towards us in a dog-catching crouch. George backed away, growling a bit, but his tail was wagging. **Then he got up on his hind legs and waved his paws. There was a burst of applause.** Warty-Beak and Hedake stopped.

George looked encouraged. He lay down, then

rolled over and over across the stage, finally springing to all fours, turning his little behind round to the audience and wagging his tail. There was a much louder burst of applause and random shouts of "Wicked!", "All right!" and "Excellent!" from the crowd.

Melchior appeared at the back and borrowed Sumil's football. **He lobbed it towards George, who flicked it neatly up in the air with his back legs and caught it on his nose.** The applause from the crowd was deafening. Hedake smiled sheepishly and went back to her seat. Warty-Beak hovered, not knowing whether to stay angry or not.

Melchior was shrugging his shoulders and looking at us apologetically. Apparently, this interruption seemed to be all George's idea.

As usual, Dinah was the first one to get her head round the situation. "We'd like to thank George for dropping in to help out with our presentation," she said, nodding encouragingly at the little dog. He sat down, wagging his tail furiously, and nodded back.

"I hope it wasn't too much bother for you, I know you've got a lot of other engagements," she said to George, shaking her head this time. He shook his head too and pointed his ears out sideways. Everyone erupted with laughter.

"But we know you feel the cause of Furry Rights is sadly neglected, and you and your friends are doing everything possible to remind us that Animals Are Human Too."

She nodded very eagerly at George, who nodded back so hard it looked as if his ears would fall off, and he added a "Woof" for good measure.

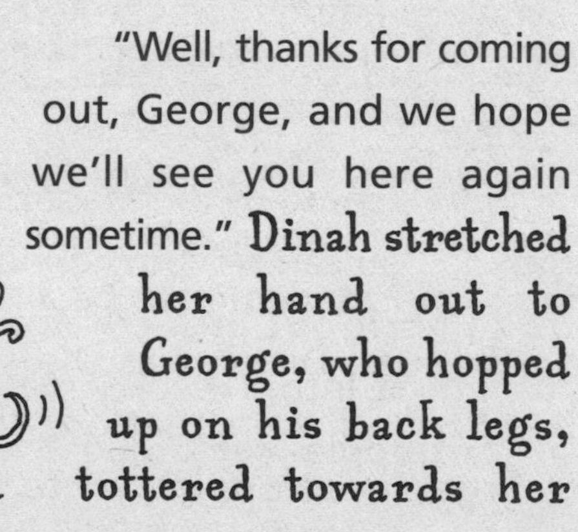

"Well, thanks for coming out, George, and we hope we'll see you here again sometime." Dinah stretched her hand out to George, who hopped up on his back legs, tottered towards her

**and extended a paw, which she shook.** Then he staggered over to Chloe and me, shook paws, dropped on to all fours and scampered off to Jolene, who greeted him with a big hug. The applause was almost loud enough to blow the walls out.

Everybody wanted to look at our table display after that. All the parents and teachers crowded round it, and lots of them came up and said, "Well done".

In actual fact, though I say so myself, our magazine was definitely the best thing of the whole evening, apart from Hannah's knitting and Sumil and Dennis's Lego. Except for George, of course.

Here's some of the magazine, not to boast, but just so you can see how good it is. I'm thinking of printing it out properly for pet owners, maybe turning it into a weekly magazine. Because even if the puppies can't read it, everyone there really liked it.

HORSOSCOPES
YOUR STARS THIS WEEK
OATIES
You have a stable period ahead.
FILLYA
A handsome stallion is near! Watch your hooves.
HOOFUS
Eat more oats
A foal may trick you
TAILO
Do not canter on Monday week
ARABINI
Your gallop of bad luck is nearly over
PEGASUS
Beware a tall dark mare
PRANCER
An apple a day keeps the donkey away
PALOMINION
Get a mane cut & hoof varnish.
SADDLO
Your perfect grooming should win the day
SKEWBALDIUS
Get in more hay for winter
CORNO
The other horse's field is not always greener
CARROTO
Enter that race -you'll win.
by Gypsy Rose Laramy
Fortuneteller to Her Majesty's Horses

# GROOMING TIPS

by Hoofella de Dapple

**BROOM** Excellent for sweeping your stable

**SAXOPHONE** The style for Musical Mares

**BUBBLES** Perfect for 'fly-away' manes

**SCRUFF** Relaxed style - Ideal for foals!

FIONA FETLOCK teaches the **SWINDLE**
The New Dance that's Sweeping Stables nationwide!

Melchior came over to us once the parents were all standing round chatting to the teachers and enjoying lots of the cheap Parents' Association drinks.

"Hope you didn't mind George joining you," he said to us out of the corner of his mouth. "Couldn't stop him. He loves Jolene, follows her everywhere."

"How does he DO all that?" I asked.

"Circus dog," Melchior said. "Got him when I was a bouncer. His trainer gave me him in exchange for letting him into a posh club. Good, innit?"

"Totally awesome," I said. "Saved the day."

At the end of the evening, Miss Hedake had a little word with us. "Well done, girls," she said. "I wouldn't say a performing dog entirely proves your point about animals having minds of their own, but it was a very entertaining presentation just the same."

"We thought so," Dinah said, nudging me.

"Excellent," Miss Hedake said, drifting off. Warty-Beak, standing nearby, smiled his sickly smile. He was about to come over, probably to

tell us that he knew, in his devilish knowing-everything way, that it had all been an accident really, when his sickly smile turned into an even more nauseating one.

We looked round and saw Lady Goodchild there, smiling radiantly at us all, even Warty. She'd obviously been looking at our display very closely.

"I particularly like this letter to the Agony Ant," Lady Goodchild said to me, pointing to the Puppies' Plea for Freedom in my magazine. "But you know, puppies do grow up quicker than children and your puppies really are old enough to leave their mum. I believe animals deserve the

respect to be free to be themselves, not like us, don't you?"

"I guess so," I said.

"Which puppy do you love the most?"

"B-Bonzo."

"How funny," said Lady G. "He is just the very one I was thinking I should leave at home with you."

I didn't mean to, I don't know how it happened. But I hugged her. All her redness seemed cosy now, like the puppies' blanket. Not scary or dragonish at all. Not a bit.

I was still dreading the next day, when Lady G was coming to collect the puppies. I was Very Extremely happy about keeping Bonzo – especially as Mum had agreed – but I couldn't bear to think how miserable Harpo would be the day her children left home.

We arranged that Dad would take Harpo out for a walk so she couldn't see them go. We persuaded Tomato to go too. I thought his wailing might be just as bad as Harpo, but little kids have short attention spans and the promise of ice cream sorted him out.

I stayed home to make sure the puppies were OK when Lady Goodchild arrived. For the first time since I realised she was kind, I wondered why she *really* wanted so many puppies, so I asked her.

"Because I have four children. And another one on the way. Haven't you noticed? But the baby will have to wait for a puppy. I'm not taking Bonzo."

I blushed. Her huge, round stomach was a baby then.

I kissed all the puppies goodbye one by one

and I didn't even cry. Much. I was thinking more about Harpo. The puppies all kissed me back in their way, but I have to admit they seemed very happy to go off with nice kind Lady G, who said we could visit any time.

Me and Mum and Bonzo spent the next half hour waiting for Harpo to come home. **We prepared a special meal of Pooch-de-luxe for her, which she never normally has as it's so expensive.** I stood by the window hugging Bonzo and waiting anxiously for her to appear.

When she did, she went straight to the puppies' basket to look for them. Then she ran upstairs. She went all round the house looking for the puppies in every room. And then, just as I thought my heart would break, she ran all round the house again, wagging her tail! She was celebrating! She had obviously had enough of motherhood.

So Lady Goodchild was right. The puppies *were* ready to leave home. And Harpo was ready to let them.

Since then I've been thinking a lot.

Lady Goodchild told me that animals are concerned with different things than humans; they don't want clothes or fame or money. She agreed that humans and animals have an equal right to freedom. But it is a different kind of freedom from ours.

I think animals and children have quite a lot in common. Children have to go to school and most of us don't want to. We would much prefer to be out playing than cooped up in a class all day pretending to learn stuff. But the main difference is that when we grow up, we get a chance to be free, but pets and circus animals and animals in zoos or on farms will never be truly free.

I've changed my mind about forcing them to do stuff they don't want. Even George, who likes performing his tricks, is a lot happier now he's out of the circus. At least, that's what Jolene thinks. I think even if animals could learn to read,

they wouldn't want to. Just helping them to be as happy as possible is the best thing. I wish adults would see that that is all children really need too.

So the puppies finally went to a really nice new home of their own and that was a Happy Ending.

On the downside, Dora went ballistic about the CDs and the oil pastels and the Barbie AND the ridiculous shoes we'd "recycled". The CDs were her favourite; she just hadn't played them yet. James Blunt. I should have known she'd like him. The shoes were a pair she'd been saving up ages for, but wasn't allowed to wear to school. The Barbie was apparently "in mint condition"

cos she'd kept it in its wrapping since she was six and it was going to be worth a fortune one day. The oil pastels were a birthday present for her best friend.

"She never brings any friends home so how was I to know she had any?" muttered Dinah. "And only Dora would think about money when she was six years old."

But the thing I felt worst about was the books. Dora had really loved those. They were her favourite books when she was little. She'd wanted to keep them for her own kids one day. I have favourite books I keep too, so I knew how she felt.

We put a poster up hoping they'd be returned, so maybe they will. Meanwhile all my pocket money goes into a Dora fund. And a digital-camera fund. Oh, yeah, and a dry-cleaning fund for Mum's best suit.

MISSING BOOKS!
Dogger
Peepo
Frog & Toad
Peter Rabbit
PLEASE RETURN!

I keep a bit of pocket money for Fidoburgers though, as I am responsible for feeding Bonzo.

It's worth it to know I'll always hear his soft sweet snore.

# Trixie

## And the Dream Pony of Doom

**ROS ASQUITH**

Hi, Trixie here!

Did you know that the thing I've always wanted most in the world is a pony? It's my biggest wish and dreamiest dream!

And did you ever hear the words, "Be careful what you wish for, it might come true"? It's the sort of thing my Grandma Clump says.

No, I didn't understand either. But I do now...!

www.harpercollinschildrensbooks.co.uk

## very extremely Brilliant guide to everything

## ROS ASQUITH

Hi, it's me, Trixie!

I ask questions ALL THE TIME, so I bet you do too. But what use are questions without answers? Not much use at all I say.

Have you ever wanted to know about –
Dogs? Jellyfish? Rude Noises?
Anything else?

Then my Very Extremely Brilliant Guide to Everything is just for YOU!

www.harpercollinschildrensbooks.co.uk